THE DEADLY SISTER

THE DEADLY SISTER

ELIOT SCHREFER

SCHOLASTIC INC.
New York Toronto London Auckland
Sydney Mexico City New Delhi Hong Kong

No part of this publication may be reproduced, stored in a retrieval system, or transmitted in any form or by any means, electronic, mechanical, photocopying, recording, or otherwise, without written permission of the publisher. For information regarding permission, write to Scholastic Inc., Attention: Permissions Department, 557 Broadway, New York, NY 10012.

This book was originally published in hardcover by Scholastic Press in 2010.

ISBN 978-0-545-16575-4

10 9 8 7 6 5 4 3 2 1   12 13 14 15 16 17/0
Printed in the U.S.A.   40
First paperback printing, June 2012

The text type was set in Palatino.
Book design by Elizabeth B. Parisi

For David Levithan

have always been the one to protect my sister.

I protected her when she was in fourth grade, standing down the bully who used to steal her lunch. I protected her when she was in seventh grade, yanking the hair of the girl who kept writing *slut* on her locker. I protected her when she was in eighth grade, lying to Mom and Dad when she stayed out all night. I protected her when she was in ninth grade, hiding the fact that she stole my homecoming dress money, working an extra shift to quietly earn it back. Every time my parents kicked her out, I found her and brought her home. Her behavior and her attitude kept getting worse, and each rescue got harder to pull off, but I never gave up. She'd been my best friend since she was born, and that never stopped mattering.

She was so cute when she was little. No one could stop gushing about her, our parents least of all. She was the focus of every dinner party; old ladies in grocery stores called her an angel; strangers would start conversations with her when she'd peer at them over the backs of restaurant booths. She was the spotlight sister, and I was the shadow sister. She started adventures. I cleaned them up once they became disasters.

She'd always been easily distracted, and as soon as she started school, the diagnoses began. ADHD, that kind of thing. Before then, my protectiveness had been fierce and uncomplicated. I told her I'd do anything for her, and her face would get all serious and she would solemnly repeat the words back to me. But a cold little barrier went up once doctors got involved. She was still the same sister I'd loved so much, and I still knew instinctively what she was thinking, but I stopped knowing what she was feeling. She was just as fiercely a part of me, but I was dazzled by her. I turned from an older sister to one of those mother cats you see raising a puppy, stubbornly blind to the core differences and exhausted by a creature she's driven to help and yet can't understand.

In the beginning, the drugs she took were all prescribed — until my parents thought the psychiatrists were overdoing it and cut back. That's when she started buying her own. At first, she got more of the drugs she'd already been taking, the ones she hoped would make her normal. Then she started buying any drug that made her feel good. And with these new drugs came new friends and new disasters.

She slammed her car into a light pole. The police found her partying in a construction site late at night, high out of her mind. When the school threatened academic expulsion, I vowed to find her a tutor so she could get her GED. I lied to our parents about where she got the wad of rolled-up bills they discovered in her messenger bag. I kept quiet when she pawned the china our grandmother had left our parents; they wouldn't know it was gone until they tried to set the table next Thanksgiving. Every secure thing she pried up in our lives, I quietly followed behind and glued it back down.

I might have been able to protect her forever.

Until Jefferson Andrews showed up dead.

SATURDAY, MAY 11

1.

I found his body during my Saturday run. I'd been doing a little training so I might have a prayer of making Vanderbilt's soccer team when I started in the fall. I paused a few miles in to let my dog, Cody, catch up. Once she did, she started to sniff some low-hanging branches. I stroked the wiry fur between her ears and was surprised to find her alert, staring somewhere between the razor fronds of low palms and then down to the river. I placed my hands on either side of her snout and tried to force her to look into my eyes. But Cody stayed rigid, kept looking toward the river.

When I asked her what was wrong, she started growling.

Scrambling to the bottom of that ravine was the last thing I wanted to do. But as soon as I let go of her, Cody disappeared in that direction. What else could I do but follow?

As I vaulted a fallen tree, slick green fungus rubbing onto my sweatshirt, a crashing noise came from a thicket below. I spotted Cody running the last few yards to the riverbank. There'd been an explosive thunderstorm the night before, and the river was surging a foot higher than usual; grasses and the bases of small trees were all underwater. Cody barked at something downriver, near a spot everyone at school called the Bend.

After I'd gone a few feet, I saw a bright orange wind-breaker, blue stripes at the elbows. It was mostly submerged, but the sleeves were hitched on to an exposed root, the jacket puffy and full of water and mud.

I edged around the riverbank to get a better view. It sounds stupid, but I called out "Hello?" — I guess to see if anyone was around and watching.

Cody began to bark again, sharp rhythmic lashes in the still air. I stalled, then got close enough to confirm that in the jacket was a body.

I put my hand over my mouth. The scene seemed both real and unreal. Done and undone. Happening and not really happening.

I didn't want to look any closer. But I had to.

It was Jefferson Andrews, unmistakably. His jawline angled toward the sky. His thick, curly hair tangled around his face.

But he wasn't saying anything.

He wasn't breathing.

He was the opposite of alive. A word I took a moment to get to, because with it came the full reality.

Dead.

A surge in the current buckled me. Shaking with cold and horror, I half swam, half dragged myself to his side. His face was so pale that no blood could possibly be flowing in him. A thick scab mottled his hair, sent crimson tendrils along his forehead. He had bled heavily before he died. He might have been dead before he hit the water, even. I went into emergency mode, forcing myself to be calm and distant, like a veteran doctor able to handle the sight of any body. I bent in closer. Whispered his name. Got no reply.

The river had parted the windbreaker. Waves pulled at the stray black hairs at the base of his muscular throat; grit from the riverbed speckled his flesh black and red. I wanted to reach out and wipe away the dirt, and almost touched my fingers to his dead skin. He was still hand-some, just . . . tired. He looked tired beyond the range of the living. Then I saw that the speckles were fire ants. One had its pincers in the smooth plane below his cheekbone, slashing through the water-softened flesh. I looked down instinctively and saw ants swarming my feet. They were bit-ing my ankles, where my wet socks had fallen down. I didn't feel them.

I didn't know whether to leave him or pull him onto the shore. The humane thing to do would have been to bring him onto land. But already I was thinking in terms of evidence.

Plus, it was so hard to see him like this. Dead like this. Handsome boys take hits in baseball games, twist and crum-ple to the roar of a disbelieving crowd. They get cancerous blood and inspire vigils around the flagpole. They're last seen waving out of sunroofs, punch cups in hand. They run out of strength trying to bust in the windows of sinking cars. Heavy-limbed and straight-backed, they take flights in camouflaged planes and never return.

I couldn't help but think: *Boys like Jefferson don't die like this.* Slammed on the head, left to bleed and drown.

The horizon narrowed, and all I could see was the rocky soil where Cody paced, her barks unrelenting.

Something there caught my eye. Half embedded in the mud, an old phone, pink with edges rubbed gray. Crowned by a telltale puffy kitten sticker.

My sister's phone.

I should say that I wasn't entirely surprised to find it. I knew she'd come to this area last night. I knew she'd been looking for Jefferson. She'd rushed off as soon as I'd told her I'd heard he was meeting up with some girl here.

She'd made a big mistake going. And even bigger mistakes after, it seemed.

Since Jefferson was dead . . .

And my sister had been here . . .

I knew what conclusion people would reach.

I splashed across the river, quick gasping screams coming from my mouth. I grabbed the phone and scrambled up the side of the ravine, my muddy sneakers dragging through the underbrush. My dog was running circles around me. Tight, protective, hysterical.

I knew Jefferson should have been my priority.

But he was already dead.

Maya, though — Maya was alive.

And in trouble.

It was time for me to play the protector again. It was time for me to go through the motions of saving her.

Because I had to. I simply had to.

Her phone was at the scene of the crime, but no one had seen it there but me. How could she be so stupid as to leave it? I remembered what she'd been like last night, drugged and emotional, totally out of her mind. She was probably holed up somewhere now, in a park or on the street. Not knowing who to turn to, her phone and all the numbers in it gone.

I had to find her.

She couldn't refuse my help this time.

I was all she had left.

2.

Jefferson Andrews had never treated my sister well.

You'd have thought he would've been a great influence on her. Valedictorian. Co-captain of the debate team. One of the stars of the swim team. Winner of Mr. Cougar, the school's goofy beauty pageant. The first invite to any party. Unendingly loyal to his friends. I proposed him when Maya needed some tutoring to get her ready for her high school equivalency test, and my parents thought he was a great choice. His family didn't have any money, so we'd even get to feel good about giving an ambitious poor kid some spending cash.

But I knew Jefferson better than that, and I suggested him against my own better judgment. Adults loved him, sure. His friends worshipped him. But those of us who weren't in his tight circle — he toyed with us. Deigned to mess around with girls with annoying laughs or fat knees only to dump them once they started to expect anything of him . . . then got party crowds roaring with stories about his "dumb psycho stalkers." Dealt drugs, and not in a "Hey, I can score a dime bag for Saturday" way but systematic, felony-level stuff, with a network of runners within the school to do his bidding and take the fall. Heavier stuff, too, like coke and speed. He knew that adults wouldn't suspect him — he manipulated his superstar image into the perfect cover.

My mom welcomed him into our house with arms wide open. Hugged him and thanked him profusely when he first arrived to tutor Maya. Set up a pitcher of lemonade at the dining room table, two ladybug glasses, legal pads and freshly sharpened pencils. Maya was seated at the far end, at first unwilling to be tutored at all, and then mortified to have someone so hot ordered to help her to learn.

It was a thrill to have Jefferson Andrews in my house — I won't deny it. I'd concoct reasons to walk past the dining room, once (daringly, or so I thought) wearing a bikini top. He didn't ever look at me. But I looked at him. I couldn't help it. Forearms cut and biceps tan, face strong and skin soft, always smiling in a teasing, arrogant way, as if amazed at the world's capacity to keep him amused. Perfectly long, perfectly lean, perfectly rosy, perfectly at ease.

And, Maya would come to learn, perfectly cruel. Those first few tutoring sessions he'd circle her wrist with his fingers as she drew a radius, would stare into her eyes while she read a passage, drinking her in so hungrily that she'd be blushing by the end. She resisted him at first — he was so unlike any guy she'd ever have gone for, way too clean-cut and preppy. She confided in me that he'd asked her out but she'd said no. The very next session he was all business, barely even said hello. I spied from the hall, saw her get tearful when he snapped that she didn't have what it took to pass the test.

The next session, she was the one placing her fingers on his wrist. Suddenly, she began trying to win him back, without ever having wanted him in the first place. She'd spent the next few weeks like that, panicked and anxious and dizzy, assuming she was in love. That was how Jefferson worked — he steered and positioned the people around him, without their ever realizing it.

My mom was euphoric about the whole situation, because Maya was finally learning something. But my dad is wiser than my mom in many ways — or at least warier. Jefferson was so polite and adult with them, always asking whether they'd had a good day and if they had an opinion about the candidates for town commissioner. Mom was charmed off her head, but Dad's hackles went up. Once after a tutoring session, Jefferson mentioned noticing the heart medication on the counter and offered to introduce my dad to swimming, because it had done such wonders for his own dad's blood pressure. Dad grunted a no. At dinner, Mom said she thought Jefferson had been so sweet to have said that, but Dad just growled and said, "Something's off with that kid." Before I could intervene, Maya flipped and said that of course it would work that way, that the moment she found someone she could actually learn with, Dad would try to sabotage it. Dishes were hurled into the sink, then there was yelling all up and down the house. The usual Maya-Dad routine.

I totally got what my dad was feeling, though. Jefferson

had snooped and then used the information he'd gained to worm in closer. It wasn't right.

Soon, the tutoring sessions had moved down to Maya's room, and just happened to be scheduled at times when our parents weren't around. I warned Maya to watch herself, but she preferred to watch him instead. I started to make sure I wasn't around, either, so all I had to deal with was the aftermath — Maya insecure, Maya ecstatic, Maya needing me to get her contraceptives because all the local pharmacists knew her a little too well.

It's not as though Maya thought she was the only girl Jefferson was sleeping with. Everyone knew that Rose Nelson, our student government president, was the only one of Jefferson's conquests who got to officially call herself "girlfriend." But there were plenty of others. Even someone as outside the important gossip circles as me knew that. Still, Maya let herself be stolen from under my parents' noses, crept out the front door when she heard Jefferson's car roll down our block at a predetermined nighttime hour. Powerless to stop her, I watched her disappear inside. She'd always have a messenger bag with her, the same bag I saw her dealing pot from after school.

I worried about her so much. It was so obvious that he was waiting for the most dramatic moment to pull the rug away, to see her love for him proven through tears and screams. I'd seen it happen with him time and again. I tried to warn Maya, but she wouldn't listen.

The more I tried to get her to give him up, the deeper into his arms I pushed her. I told her about Cara Johnson, whose parents caught her carving Jefferson's name into her arm and sent her away to rehab. I told her about Donna Meadows, who made the mistake of telling Rose that Jefferson had slept with her, only to get a slap from Rose and a cold-turkey cutoff from Jefferson. I pointed out Rachael McHenry, who told Jefferson she'd given up her virginity to him only to hear him say, "Well, I wish I could give it back."

"None of that's true," she'd tell me, and I had to wonder if she had any notion of what was true anymore.

Now Jefferson had set his sights on my family, and all I could do was get prepared to clean up the mess. Little did I know that the mess would be Jefferson Andrews himself.

3.

I knew I didn't have much time. Even though few people ran in this area, I couldn't count on Jefferson's body going undiscovered for long. I had to get to Maya right away.

There was no way to call her — her phone was in my hand. But I'd try her friends. I'd find out which house she was crashing at, which bar or mall parking lot she'd passed out in. It was a start. I would come to know everything Maya knew, and then I'd make a plan. By now the routine of tracking her down and dragging her to safety was familiar to me. Though this time so much more depended on my pulling everything off.

"What's up, guys?" — many of Maya's friends' voice mails picked up this way, like their phone calls lit up the power grid so brightly that they had to answer in the plural — "This is Ranya. I guess I'm not by my phone, so leave a message."

"What's up, guys? Leave a message."

"Guys, meet David's cell phone. David's cell phone, meet the guys. Converse amongst yourselves."

"You've reached Jefferson Andrews —" I pulled the phone away from my ear, as if stung. I'd been going alphabetically down the list and had stopped looking at who I was dialing.

"What's up, guys? You haven't reached Katie, so leave a message."

Then, finally, "Hello?"

"Oh!" I said. "Who's this?" I glanced at the screen, but it just read *Medusa*.

"Who's *this*? Maya?"

My voice came out sounding amazingly calm. "No, it's her sister. I'm looking for Maya. Is she around?"

"Why would she be here?" Whoever this was, his tone was really defensive. I sat up.

"Um, who is this?"

A pause. "Keith. Why are you calling from her number?"

"Okay, Keith. I don't have time to explain all of it to you. I just need to find her. Can you help me?"

"This is really something. You think I'm going to help you, just like that?"

I thought I heard heartbreak, a history of fights and wounds in his voice. I recognized it all too well. "I don't know what's passed between the two of you," I said. "Honestly, I don't. And I'm not trying to poke around. I just —" I let out a long sigh. "Thanks, anyway."

I didn't hang up — I'd long ago decided never to be the one to end a call, to always let the other person be through with me first. Funny thing was, though, Keith didn't hang up either. Maybe he had the same idea. I spent a few seconds listening to the line, to the sounds of traffic and clinking dishes on the other end. I crouched at the roadside, a bead of perspiration running through the sweat-salt on my temple and landing on my shorts.

"Is she okay?" Keith finally asked. He had a high voice. I imagined him in skinny gray jeans, a cigarette behind his ear. In my mind he was not only gesturing with his hands but with his whole arms flailing over his head — a high-strung kid.

"I don't know," I said. "Look, if you don't know where she is, then I have to go."

"Medusa's Den," he said.

"I'm sorry?"

"Medusa's Den. The tattoo place on Langdell. She came by last night to get a tattoo covered up. She crashed at my place above the studio. You can start here. I have to run some errands, but you can come by once I'm back.

"Thanks. Thanks a lot."

"I won't be back until four, though."

"Great, thanks. Hurry, if you can."

"I might be there when you see her. So you know."

"Um, okay."

"It's a shock, talking to Abby Goodwin. We haven't met, of course. But finally talking to Maya's mythical, straight-edge sister. Some rule just got broken, you know what I mean?"

"Bye, Keith."

I broke my rule after all and finished the call. The End

button beeped for a while before I realized I hadn't let it go. Maya's phone tight in one hand, I rubbed my sweat from the screen with the sleeve of my sweatshirt.

Back home, my parents would be beginning their lazy Saturday routine. Chairs groaning against floorboards, the low hum of public radio, water spraying against the hollow spot of the porcelain sink. I hadn't seen them yet today. That was normal enough — I usually spent my Saturday mornings doing homework in the library, running, and eventually driving over to my best friend Cheyenne's for gossip and bagels. Part of me wanted to go straight home, let my parents see how pale I was and hear them ask what was wrong. Then I'd tell them. What to do next would become their responsibility. But their hysterical reactions . . . I couldn't stand the thought of the scene they'd make. For now, all they knew was that their youngest daughter hadn't come home. Not at all unusual for Maya. Once my parents knew more, though, my sister would become a potential killer. My mother might have listened to my reasoning, but my father would insist on calling the police immediately. Always "the truth will set you free" with him. But we'd never faced anything like this. If they pinned this on Maya, it would get her jailed. Or executed.

But I couldn't think about that. I had to focus on saving her.

I had to believe she'd have a reason prepared, or an alibi. If asked, she'd have something to say.

But would it be enough?

Knees cracking, I stood and started sprinting. Cody lurched to her feet, grunted in complaint.

Home was four miles off. Too far.

In order to get to Maya, I needed a car. And in order to get a car, I needed someone I could trust.

And in my life, that meant Cheyenne.

4.

My town is an overheated stretch of cracked pavement in the middle of an alligator-hunted wasteland between Naples and Miami. We have three high schools, whose athletic competitions are the focus of an otherwise bored and sluggish community. The Sunday outing for most is a trip to Walmart, or Target if they're classy. We've got some tension between the haves and have-nots, I guess, but it's not like there are any private schools — it's just that some people were born and raised locally and live in mobile homes, and others buy brushed-steel appliances in Miami and live around here because there are more golf courses. That's all there is to know about my town. If you were driving through you'd only stop as long as it took to buy a soda. I recommend turning left off the highway and going to Ernie's gas station, across from the high school, then getting back on I-75 heading anywhere else.

It was an easy run to the mall. Cheyenne was halfway through her shift at Denim Jungle, not quite busy folding wide-leg jeans. "Whoa," she said when she saw me, "what the hell is up?"

Was my flipping out that obvious?

"I need your help," I said.

"Yeah, you do!" she said with a smirk.

She gave some excuse to her manager. He shook his head, then spied me lingering at the store entrance and, tipped off to the freakish need I was projecting, reluctantly nodded. Cheyenne and I went to the food court. It was great to be alone with her. My best friend. Her skin tight and splotchy, masses of dry hair and the going-hunting look of the only recently skinny. She watched me as she took long drags from a Manchu Wok Diet Coke.

I explained everything.

Or rather, I explained everything I was willing to have the world at large know: basically, that I'd gone running and discovered Maya's phone in the woods. I couldn't put words to what had happened to Jefferson. The arms emerging from the water, as if to pull himself up and out. The windbreaker parachuting with water. The sharp jaws of those feeding ants. I knew Cheyenne would be horrified that I hadn't called the police yet, that I hadn't even told my parents. So she couldn't know about Jefferson. She listened to me sympathetically, but one arched eyebrow told me she thought I was going overboard. I wanted to clutch her, to hear her reassurances that everything would work out okay. I'd spend the weeks to come wanting nothing more than that.

"So your sister boinked some guy in the woods and her phone fell out of her panties," Cheyenne said. "Or she got high and went skinny-dipping. What else is new? That cell phone has probably been left in beds all over the state."

I surprised myself by laughing. It had an iron, slashing

feeling behind it, and I had to work to make the laughter stop. Talking to Cheyenne made me feel more alive than I had all morning.

"I can't find her," I finally said.

"This is just the first time you've bothered looking for her in a while. Remember back when you actually cared, when you were still being an older sister and letting her be a toxic influence on your life? We'd drive around all night trying to find her, and she'd always turn out to be passed out on some guy's couch, or detained by security guards . . . or remember that time we thought she ran away and she'd actually just decided to hang out at the strip mall for five hours eating fro yo, getting high in bathrooms, and chatting up some random Japanese girl she met by the vending machines? She's *never* at your house, and when she is, she's in that swampy basement of a bedroom. I don't get why you're so worked up *now*, hon."

That was when I should have told her. But I couldn't tell her. Because, like everyone else, Cheyenne assumed the worst about Maya. There would be no benefit of the doubt here, and I couldn't have Cheyenne refusing to help.

"I'm really scared," I said. "I just need you to acknowledge that, all right? We aren't discussing some random girl. It's my sister."

Cheyenne laced her fingers through the wires of her chair back. "I've always been really impressed that you finally managed to cut Maya out of your life. You used to spend every weekend being her nursemaid. Driving to Orlando to pick her up because someone jacked her wallet. Shuttling to a cab driver's house with twenty bucks so he wouldn't beat her up or hike her back to Pakistan or something. And what good would it ever do? You'd get an ulcer, and she'd get back in trouble. You know, you have to respect the lesson you learned, to have the wisdom to know the difference between the things you can change and those that are just blocks to your shui."

Cheyenne loves astrology, has considered becoming a midwife, and is the primary funder of the local bookstore's self-help section. She frequently sets up cornfield mazes of mental health jargon and then gets lost in them. But the girl isn't dumb. She was in the running for valedictorian of our class. In fact, she was probably first now, with the competition half submerged in the Everglades.

"If you start letting yourself worry about Maya, you'll never stop," Cheyenne concluded. "Look at your parents. They let Maya dominate their lives, and she wrecked their marriage. Once and nearly twice."

"No, the affair wrecked their marriage," I said.

"The first time, sure."

"Whatever. I just need you to come with me to search for her," I said. "Right now. Some emo guy named Keith's waiting for me."

"I just moved up from the kids' store," Cheyenne said. "If I blow off an afternoon shift now, I'm not coming back. If you can promise me that Maya's going to cover my car payments, I'll go look for her with you."

Tears must have been standing in my eyes. Cheyenne softened. "There's more to this than you're telling me, isn't there?" she asked.

I nodded into my lap. I couldn't look at her. My best friend in the world, and I couldn't convey my panic.

"Look, I'd blow the afternoon off," she said softly, with the same tone she used when I got my dress caught on a gymnasium pegboard at the eighth-grade dance and she convinced her dad to take us out for ice cream afterward. "But I guess I don't see what you're really freaking out for. And you're talking about heading off into a totally sketch area of town. I definitely don't want you to go alone. But if you're really worried, call the police. Call your parents. Veronica. Or *my* mom, even. I just don't get why you're suddenly being Nancy Drew."

"I don't know what she's gotten herself into. I have to find out exactly what it is before I potentially screw up her future."

"You're too good to people who don't give a crap about you, you know that?"

There were sweeter friends I could have turned to. Ones who would be hugging me, who would see the depth of my hurt even if they didn't know the cause. Who would be saying tons of things that would make me feel better, rather than these edgy little truths. But more than comfort, I was craving honesty.

I took a deep breath. "It's Jefferson Andrews," I said.

"What do you mean, it's Jeff Andrews?" No one but Cheyenne ever called him Jeff. I guess she wanted to diminish him. Make him more masterable, somehow. "It's Jeff Andrews who was off in the woods with her?"

I nodded. Suddenly, it felt like if I didn't get some truth out right away, I wouldn't ever be able to speak, about anything, ever again. So I spoke.

"He's dead."

Nothing changed in the food court. A baby was still climbing on the back of a nearby seat. The Miss Sakura girl, wearing a skirt as a shirt, was still handing out samples. I could still hear the hum of the refrigerators at the cookie cake place. Cheyenne was still in the same position. But I witnessed something change in her. Her life had entered the same twilight realm as mine.

She didn't ask if I was kidding. She saw the answer in my face.

I didn't want to give her space to speak, didn't want to hear her tell me I was accountable and monstrous. So I rambled on about the physical details. The run and the dog. The bashed head. The blood and the phone.

"He's really dead," Cheyenne said, finally.

I nodded.

"And you think your sister had something to do with it?"

I couldn't answer that. I was cold and sweating, like I'd just woken up in the middle of the night with a fever. Even within the astonishment of finally revealing myself, I couldn't shake the feeling that Cheyenne wasn't totally sur-prised to hear Jefferson was dead. She'd gone glassy, and her pupils were huge, but she hadn't flinched.

"You're right not to have gone to your parents," she said softly. "They gave up on Maya long before you did. They might actually *want* her caught. So that they'd finally, offi-cially, not have to deal with her anymore."

I nodded solemnly. I'd drawn the same conclusion, even though I hadn't admitted it to myself until now. I wanted to thank her, suddenly, for saying it out loud.

"We'll go to that tattoo place first," she said. "Medusa something? Then we'll try Veronica's. She's the only sorta parental type that gives a crap about Maya anymore — if your sister's going to go to an adult for help, and I bet she will, it'll be her. But maybe, do you think . . . oh god, Abby. What if Maya doesn't realize she's killed him? Like they fought, and she left without knowing he was bleeding to death?"

I nodded.

When Cheyenne tossed her Diet Coke into the trash, it traced a zigzag in the air, thrown by a shaky hand. Otherwise she seemed totally in control, someone I could lean all my weight on. "We'll take my car," she said, as though I hadn't arrived on foot, as though we had some other option.

She didn't tell her manager she was leaving. She just tossed her work ID into the trash as we left the mall.

Once we pushed out of the front doors I untied Cody, who had fallen asleep with her head resting against a bike rack, and started walking to Cheyenne's car. Maya's phone buzzed in my pocket. The text was from Keith.

abby made it back early im here if u want to come.

My fingers flew over the keys.

ill be there in half an hour with a friend. dont tell anyone were coming.

5.

As we sat at a traffic light, I felt a new tightness in my stomach and realized that I hadn't eaten all day. Cheyenne kept energy bars in the glove compartment, but I couldn't imagine taking any food in. My stomach felt vacuumed shut, as if anything I'd force myself to chew and swallow would sit on the sealed organ until it wandered back up to my mouth.

This isn't me, I thought as Cheyenne merged onto the interstate. *I'm the one who convinces the group not to jump Thrill Hill, who goes to every party but leaves early and never throws a single one of her own. I'm not the one to get wrapped up in a murder and not call the police. To willfully start down a chain of wrong.*

I watched her go through the mundane activity of clicking on her turn signal, inching forward, and stopping as she waited for traffic to clear enough for us to merge. When we jerked to an especially hard stop and Cheyenne started yelling at a driver, a key on a necklace fell from beneath the collar of her shirt. Cheyenne noticed me staring at her and tucked the key away. "You know, if you'd told me that someone I knew was going to die," she said, in that bizarre singsong she uses when she's struggling to make conversation, "I'd have predicted Jeff Andrews."

It was a hugely weird thing to say, weird enough to make me cancel the question I was about to ask about the key. I didn't reply for a few seconds. "Everyone loves Jefferson," I said, in the manner of a television announcer.

"He wasn't a nice boy," Cheyenne said, tapping her finger against the steering wheel.

The neighborhoods around Xavier High are all planned developments in soil shades, the monotony broken only by electronics stores or billboarded restaurants where the silverware comes wrapped in waxy paper. But Medusa's Den is deeper into the old town, near the abandoned rail depot in the center. Surrounded by drifters and gangs of kids avoiding home. Cheyenne locked the doors as we surfed for parking. We finally found a spot in a gravel lot that spilled between office buildings. We hid our purses and watches under the seats. I pulled my hair down and mussed it. I always feel plastic downtown.

I'd been so intent on finding Maya that I hadn't really considered what I'd say to her once I was face-to-face with her again. I'd have to see what condition she was in, find out what she knew about what had happened. I imagined her frantic and scared and angry, spouting nonsense. Maybe she'd have taken something to calm her nerves, would be docile and open, all pupils and liquid limbs.

Cheyenne paid the meter, placed the receipt on her dashboard, and clicked the door lock button until the car honked twice. We headed toward Medusa's Den, my dog leading the way.

People only go to our downtown to work, so on the weekends it's a hollowed-out place, like the set of an apocalypse movie minus the zombies. Locked revolving doors, vividly empty streets, homeless asleep on curling cardboard, gravel parking lots boundaried by rusty chains. In the corner of one of the more desolate lots was a large green vintage car. I stopped in my tracks.

Cheyenne pulled up short alongside me. "What — oh, shit."

We stared at the car. Cody whined.

"How'd he get his car here, if he's dead in the woods?" Cheyenne asked.

"Well, somebody obviously must have put it here."

"Who would ride off with Jeff's car?"

I couldn't avoid stating the obvious implication. "Who do you think?"

"Abby, this really doesn't look good for her. Not at all."

"I know," I snapped.

"What do we do about the car?"

"We stop standing here staring at it. Let's go."

"I think we should investigate it," Cheyenne said.

"*No.*" I was shaking. Cheyenne took my hand and squeezed it.

Medusa's Den was right around the corner. It was a blacked-out window next to a liquor store where people placed orders from behind a Plexiglas wall. The grimy door hummed with neon. I pulled it open.

The walls, floor, and much of the ceiling were plywood.

In a case, body-piercing jewelry — much of it glowing green, yellow, orange — glinted like tropical fish next to some truly ugly fluorescent bongs. Two girls on a ripped couch by the entrance had just said something that ended with "Okay, Mama."

"How do I find Keith?" I asked them.

They glanced at each other to see who should go first. I was irritated by the delay and, obscurely, by the very fact that these girls might have been friends of my sister. If I was the one to spend so much of my life looking after her, didn't I at least deserve to know everyone she knew?

"You wait around," one said.

"So you know, we were here first," said the other with a smirk.

"We don't need tattoos," I said. "I just have to talk to him. Do you know which studio is his?"

"He's probably upstairs," said the first girl. "He lives here." She thumbed toward the back of the parlor. "I like your dog."

I cautioned myself as I climbed the stairs: *Don't act like you suspect Maya, or she won't let you help.* My throat tightened.

Keith — and this guy could only be Keith — opened the door. Not a gawky emo boy after all. A long history of ink on his body. Predictable tattoos in the predictable places (a girl on a bicep, a skull on a calf) in faded ink, and fresher and more unusual images in more unusual places. A type-writer on the inside of his elbow. A planet on the corded muscle that led into his boxers. He was wearing only those boxers.

The tattoos were too plentiful and too engrossing. The door had been open for rich seconds and I hadn't said a thing.

Say something.

He was a warrior, something from a dreamscape.

Say something.

A snake vined through the paisley on his shoulder, its tongue licking toward his earlobe.

"I'm Cheyenne and this is Abby," Cheyenne said, pushing past me. "The dog's name is Cody."

"You look just like Maya," Keith said to me as he reached out a hand to fend off Cody, who was in full greeting mode. No one ever said I looked like Maya. Flirting cashiers called us cousins, and even that was a stretch. We had the same body type; that was it.

"I'm sorry?" I said.

"*'I'm sorry?'*" Keith echoed back in a mocking accent that might have been aiming at British. A moment came back to me: getting into the family car, Maya calling me affected. I hadn't known what the word meant, but I knew what it felt like and argued back hotly. Maya had only stared at me from her half of the backseat. *I have something on you. I am larger. I reach further.*

"Abby Goodwin and Co.," Keith said. "Come in."

It was a busy, dirty loft space, more an attic than an apartment. But clean light streamed in, illuminating Keith's ink.

He turned and sauntered into the room, not bothering to look back. In Maya's world, assumptions were good enough. Keith was hardly concerned whether Cheyenne and I felt welcome.

He plucked a limp collared shirt from the back of a chair and shrugged it on. A sea turtle disappeared under the neckband. The tattoos were strategic: When he turned around with the shirt on, none of them were visible.

"Is Maya here?" I asked.

"It's a small space," Keith said. "What you see is all there is."

I did a quick scan. One door, hanging open, led to a bathroom. The rest of the loft was cluttered, full of hidden corners. I glanced in a wastepaper basket next to me and then wished I hadn't. There was a blue bandage on top, blood leaking from an oval in the center and sealing one side in a crimson line. It looked like a used pad. Cody already had her nose halfway into the basket. I yanked her back.

Keith noticed my reaction. "That's your sister's, actually. She had me do a tattoo cover-up last night. It bled more than usual, but that's probably because her skin was still sensitive from the original. She only got it a few weeks ago."

"What time was that?" I asked. "The cover-up, I mean."

"Early evening. Eight, maybe?"

There were other things I should have asked about, but I couldn't get my brain to put events in order. Cheyenne stepped in. "Did she stay the night?" she asked.

"I'm not sure she'd want me to give her sister that kind of information."

"What's that supposed to mean?" I asked.

"You want something to drink? I've got, um, water or bourbon. No? Suit yourself. All I mean is that you two aren't exactly the closest of sisters. I can't imagine that's news to you." Keith pulled out a pair of chairs — puffy brown brass ones, like from the "Wait to be Seated" area of a diner — and motioned that we should sit. We did. I balanced forward on the balls of my feet.

We *were* close sisters. It also just so happened that she hated me. "I've got her phone," I said, brandishing it. The move felt lame, like I was trying to prove a connection to her.

"She hates phones. I've heard the rants. I'm sure she's not suffering without it."

"Look, she's in trouble. She needs help. You said she was here — so where is she?"

Keith laughed. "She's not in trouble. She's doing fine."

"When did you last see her?"

"She spent last night here."

"Really?" Cheyenne asked.

"Did she seem okay?" I asked.

He smirked. "Why, Little Miss Goodwin, wouldn't she seem okay?"

I could tell he knew something I didn't. But how to make him reveal it?

"I need you to tell me," I said. "Please."

"Maya's a good friend of mine. And I know she goes to great pains to make sure that her family doesn't know where she is. So unless you cough up a better reason, I'd say it's time for you to go."

All I wanted to do was talk to her. Why was that so hard? With any other sister, it would have been simple. But I couldn't go telling everyone it looked like my little sis had killed her drug dealer sex-boy.

"I know," I said, clearing my throat, "that Maya and I aren't too close anymore. I know she avoids me and my parents, that she might tell you she hates us. She's probably involved in all sorts of things she'd be furious if any of us found out about. But she's my *sister*, and something's come up that makes it so important that I find her. I can't explain it to you, but you have to know that I really need to do this. I'm not trying to get her in trouble. I'm trying to save her."

Keith lit a cigarette and stared at the tip. Never taking his eyes from the glowing point, he held the pack out to me and Cheyenne, placing it in his shirt pocket when we both declined. A shirt cuff fell back on his arm, and I saw beneath it a second cuff tattooed directly onto his flesh, complete with cuff link.

"Maya," he called, "your sister is here."

6.

She was thirteen the first time she ran away. That evening I'd been doing dishes while listening to my parents scold her for skipping school. As I soaped a plate, it struck me: She'd said nothing to any of us for a week. She'd accepted my parents' waves of frustration, but it was like we were a radio station and the technology didn't work both directions. She'd stopped broadcasting anything back.

I followed their lecture as it inevitably turned toward her failing schoolwork and lousy friends. *I'll stay flexible*, I told myself. *I'll try not to judge. I'll be the one she's still willing to talk to.* I knew she was barely sleeping anymore, that she spent her evenings reading magazines in the basement or watching TV on her computer. I set my alarm for one A.M., when I knew our parents would be long asleep. I went to the kitchen and made peppermint hot chocolate, her childhood favorite. I poured two cartoon-kitten mugs full and headed downstairs.

Back during the divorce year, Maya and I had fixated on those kitten mugs. We'd used them constantly, filling them with orange juice at breakfast, water at lunch, and milk at dinner. They always went to their special spot in the dishwasher, mine in the back and hers nestled right next to it. We'd take them to the roof and sip and talk, or on weekend mornings we'd walk around the neighborhood with steaming tea. On those walks she'd ask question after question about why our parents were splitting, even though I never had any answers. One morning, I made a plan with Dad to meet at the local fields to go over some soccer moves. I waited for him for an hour, until who came huffing down the street but little Maya, clutching two kitten mugs of gone-cold chocolate. She didn't need to explain: In the emotional torture they were putting themselves through that year, my parents forgot appointments all the time. Maya had had plans to go camping with her best friend's family that weekend, and she missed out just so she could come console me with those watery cold chocolates. We huddled together on the edge of the field, my shoulder against hers, and I was so glad that my otherwise annoying eleven-year-old sister had totally come through when it mattered most.

Two years later, I walked down those basement stairs intending to return the favor. I meant to convince her to stay, to make her feel like she belonged. But she was already gone. I've never been able to shake the feeling that everything since has been my fault.

I wouldn't have thought anyone could have hidden in Keith's bed, but here she was, emerging from the stale airspace beneath the comforter. The sheets must have gone weeks without being made, their wrinkles thickened into deep ridges. She cringed in the pale light. It struck me that maybe she wasn't avoiding me; she was just embarrassed to have been found in this guy's slimy bed. She hit the ground unsteadily, jostling a side table and spilling empty prescription bottles that pinged and rolled on the floor.

"What are you doing here?" she asked. The emphasis was on *you*, like she couldn't care less about my reasons — it was my very presence that had her pissed. "What exactly are you trying to save me from?"

She moved into the brighter light of the window, which cast her green. She hadn't slept in a long time — the skin beneath her eyes was rumpled. She looked like she'd just dodged a speeding car that was turning around for another pass: unsteady, panicked. But did she look all messed up because she'd just killed someone, or because that was the way she always looked? Both our fates would hang on what people decided was the answer.

Every time I saw her, I tried to find the little girl underneath.

Every time I saw her, I failed.

Maya liked to wear a lot of pink and a lot of black. Her panties sported both colors, in tight horizontal stripes. Her thighs looked red and sore. I was embarrassed that Cheyenne was seeing my sister like this. And I was angry that Maya had waited for Keith's permission to come out. She was passive, easily led — another way we were different.

"Hey, Cody," she murmured. The dog had found a stretch of her exposed heel and begun to nuzzle.

"Is there someplace private where Maya and I can talk?" I asked.

Keith looked at Maya. "Take my studio. I'm not using it until four."

Cheyenne followed Maya and me downstairs, then squeezed my arm, said "I'll meet you outside," and kept moving toward the front. Cody reluctantly allowed herself to be dragged behind her.

The plywood wall shuddered as Maya closed us into the studio. A tattoo needle droned next door, cut off, then droned again.

"So this is where you spend all your time?" I asked.

"One of the places," Maya said. She eased herself onto the tattooing table, paper crinkling under her. She was still in her underwear, though she'd thrown on one of Keith's T-shirts to cover her breasts. It had a chicken on it, of all things. I wheeled away a cart with needles and little tubs of ink, took the artist's chair. Maya clutched one of her elbows, a forearm across her belly. It was an insecure and intimidating pose, making it look like she was both closing herself off and preparing to use her arm as a club. Even clutching her bicep, her fingers shook. It made the grayer skin near her elbow quiver. She was so thin. Effortlessly, sickly thin. Like a model, or someone soon to be deceased.

"No one can hear us, right?" I said.

Maya nodded, eyes still suspicious.

"Jefferson Andrews," I said.

She flinched. "What about Jefferson Andrews?"

"He's dead."

There it was again, the godlike moment of changing the

currents of someone's life. Every time I said he was lying dead at the bottom of the ravine, there was a rush and a jump and the universe changed. Maya's outline went hazy for a moment.

She didn't go pale — she couldn't have gotten paler — but a sheen appeared on her skin. She was horrified. But she didn't look surprised. Not quite.

"Tell me you didn't kill him, Maya," I said.

"I didn't kill him."

"Why don't you tell me what happened?"

"What happened? What do you mean?" It wasn't really a question. It was a bid for time. I waited.

"Maya. Only I know." I left out Cheyenne, to keep my allegiances uncomplicated. I could lose Maya's trust — whatever trust she had for me — so easily. "But someone else could be finding his body right now. We don't have time. I need you to tell me exactly what happened last night."

She was scared now. Calculations passed just beneath her face. What I'd told her about Jefferson, perhaps slowed by drugs in her bloodstream, seemed to hit in slow motion. She staggered to her feet. "He's not dead!"

"I *found him*, Maya. And he *is* dead. Drowned, or hit on the head. Dead." I felt sick and full at the same time.

"Where is he?"

"In the river. Right below where you met up with him last night. *Did you hit him?*"

"He was there to meet up with some other girl. But when I got there, she wasn't there. I was confused."

40

"Start at the beginning. I was the one who told you he was with some other girl, remember? And you went to find him. Did you talk to him?"

"Yeah. Oh my god. He's not dead, Abby. He can't be." She twisted her arms together. Her torso hinged so she almost folded, left over right. I put my arm around her shoulders. It was the first time I'd touched her in a long time. She smelled like her room smells: that gasoline stench of old rolling papers; a potent, almost buttery pungency of candy; and cheap berry perfume. But she also smelled of clues to the other half of her life: invisible, unknowable, a challenge to the imagination. Chemical smells, unhealthy sweat. Drug vapors. Somewhere deep in the fibers of her shirt, she smelled like burnt detergent. I pulled her tighter, until she slipped free.

She began hitting herself. The heels of her hands made soft thunks against her skull. I grabbed her wrists and pulled her arms down to her side. She was gorgeous for a moment. Gorgeous and otherworldly and profoundly ill.

"Look, Maya," I said. "You're going to tell me everything that happened last night, and then we're going to figure out what to do."

She didn't nod. She just stared from the hollows of her face. Right then, I wouldn't have been surprised if she'd passed out or bolted from the room. I had no idea what to expect.

"For right now," I continued, "you need to get grieving for Jefferson out of your head. Pretend he's still alive. Deal with that later. Your life is on the line, okay? Our priority is deciding what the police will think, and what that means for you."

At the mention of the police, a glass was lifted. She nodded, ran her tongue over her craggy lips. "Someone saw him parked at the Bend. So I went. I knew he was waiting for a girl to meet up with him. He'd met up with me there plenty often."

We'd been over this the night before. I was used to this frustration — Maya never quite seemed to be listening to me, asked only the most basic questions, regularly requested information I'd given her moments earlier. It told me, over and over, that she didn't really care what I had to say. And whenever I asked, *Did you hear what I just said?*, she turned defensive. It's weird that I was swelling with irritation even as something so serious was happening, but so be it.

"So you went to the Bend . . ." I prompted.

Maya nodded, and I watched her get temporarily lost in the details of the room: the paper on the table, the tubes and contraptions and wrapped needles. Her mouth was hanging open. She snapped it shut and shivered, rubbing her arms.

"Was he there?" I asked.

"Yeah. His car was there. I rode in on my bike. I remember his taillights glowing. Smoke coming from the tailpipe. I banged on the hood, to freak out whatever girl was inside. But when he rolled down the foggy window, I saw it was just him. He had a joint, was listening to music on the car stereo. I got in and closed the door. Automatic reaction, you know."

"He must have been surprised to see *you* get in."

She kept going, like I hadn't spoken. "He was just sitting there, I guess waiting for that girl to arrive. And he flipped when he saw it was me, just flipped. 'Oh, what are you doing here? Me, I'm just hanging out,' that kind of typical crap. Exactly how I'd have expected him to act if I caught him cheating. I told him to cut through it and tell me what he was really doing there. What he was planning on doing with Caitlin. He kept telling me not to be ridiculous, instead of saying he wasn't meeting anyone. So I knew I was right." Her voice kept rising, like she was back there all over again. Maybe the drugs were actually aiding the confession.

"Who's Caitlin?" I asked. "I didn't mention a Caitlin. I'd just heard it was some girl."

"He'd mentioned her to me once. Said I had a nice ass, but not as nice as Caitlin's. So I knew. That name stuck with me. How could I forget it? I mean, it's not like I didn't know he was sleeping with other girls. But I guess I hadn't had to face it before, straight out like that. He told me to calm down. I was really upset. He started kissing me. I can't believe he did that, tried to kiss me when I was so worked up."

You kissed him back, I thought, *and you know it. No one resists him.*

"He locked the doors and dove into the backseat. Just *expecting* me to follow. It got me mad again, and I started thinking about some slut with a great ass named Caitlin arriving, so I threw open the door. He tried to pull me back, but I slipped out of the car. He whipped out of the driver's side and leaned over the hood. He was furious, called me a tease and a bitch. 'It's not Caitlin,' he finally said, and he started *smiling*. Like he was getting off seeing me tortured. I asked him who it was, and he wanted to know what it was worth if he told me. I said I couldn't believe he was asking *me* for favors after everything else he'd done, and that was when he confessed he'd been planning on meeting up with another girl, but that he didn't really like her and it was just to get her off his back. I didn't believe him, of course, but while I was thinking about what he'd said, I let him hold me, I guess. God, what happened next? Let me think."

There was a lot to unpack out of what she was telling me, but right then I just needed to keep her talking. "So at this point you *knew* he'd been lying to you. Because at first he hadn't admitted that he was meeting some girl, and then he admitted it."

"Yes, Abby. I *knew* he was lying to me. And I was still there. Don't be such a Girl Scout."

"Just keep telling me what happened."

"God! I'm trying!" She barreled on. "So I'm standing there, and we're talking or whatever, and I keep telling him that I just want to lie down. I'm finding it hard to put sentences together, you know what I mean? He said we could just stand there and enjoy the view, even though I couldn't see anything from where we were because it was so dark, and that felt fine, just being held even by someone who I knew was playing me, but then he wanted to talk and I said can't we just stay quiet and he asked what was wrong and I said I wanted to lie down again."

"Wait, were you high?"

"Out of my mind. I thought you'd have figured that out by this point. He was practically jamming pills in my mouth."

I pictured it, Jefferson placing a little pill on his fingertip — he had these broad, rough fingers, more tools than body parts — and working his finger between Maya's lips. "Are you high right now?" I asked. I hated my tone — I sounded like a doctor again.

"No, *I'm not high right now*. So I wind up in the back of his car, lying down. He's talking to someone on the phone, and I just want to go to sleep so that when I wake up, my brain will start thinking in order again. And I guess I do fall asleep, because I wake up. I feel his hands on me, and his lips on my mouth, his tongue prying my lips open. Then it all comes back to me, that he was there waiting for some other girl, even if I sorta believed him that it wasn't Caitlin, and that if I let him keep on going, I'd never have made a choice, that entire evening. I'd have just been *led*. It was our last night together, and I would have let him do all the wrecking. Does that make sense?"

I nodded.

Maya lay back and covered her eyes. I thought she might

have been getting a headache, so I reached over and switched off the lights. "So I gave in a little, and then I shoved. I was no match for him, of course, but I guess I sort of surprised him. He sprang back and hit his head on the roof, hard, and I slipped out from under him. So I'm standing on the grass, in the glare of his headlights, and he's right in my face, telling me to leave. I'm halfway on my bike, when I suddenly get incredibly mad. It was the feeling of being sent away that did it to me. Like who's he to screw me over and then *dismiss* me? Our future was lost — there was no point being nice anymore. So I started raging."

I wondered if she was telling the truth. I'd seen her sullen plenty of times, almost constantly, actually, but never *angry*. I mostly believed it, though. She wasn't even making her usual minimal eye contact, she was that wrapped up in the moment she was describing. "He didn't know me well enough, I guess. He was surprised. I wouldn't have been able to hit him if he hadn't been surprised. But I took this whiskey bottle that someone had littered and I slammed him with it. I wanted to shock him. But the neck of the bottle was broken, I guess, and it was full of rainwater. It was so dark, I couldn't see details. So it was heavy and sharp. It was raining by then, and . . . it slipped out of my fingers. I . . . he howled. Not like mad, but like wounded. Like he was really hurt."

I nodded. I could easily picture Jefferson's rage and confusion. He was always in control. Losing that had to have been the worst part for him.

"Look at me, though," she said, her face twisted in agony. "I'm a weakling. I couldn't really kill someone. No matter how mad and high I was. I just made him bleed a little."

"That bottle must have been some weapon, Maya," I said slowly. "I saw his face. It was pretty cut up. And he looked like he fell. I don't know which killed him, the bottle or the fall."

I thought she was going to start screaming, but no sound came out. She slowly closed her mouth, wiped her lips. When she finally spoke, her voice was barely audible. "I could have stayed. I could have called for help."

"What *did* you do?" I asked.

"I left. I came here."

"So he wasn't dead when you left?"

"Abby, no! I didn't kill him! I couldn't have. Of all people, *you* have to believe me."

Of all people, you have to believe me — I'd heard this plenty of times before, usually when Maya was guilty of something. It was meant to make me feel special, connected. But I also knew she'd use it on anyone she had a use for.

"Was he on the ground when you left?" I asked.

"Yeah, on his knees. I was worried what he'd do when he got up, what he'd do to me. I had to go. I know everyone sees him as Mr. Gentleman, but when he got angry, it was scary. You understand, right?"

"You left your phone there," I said.

"I didn't mean to. I had to go home to call Keith."

"Wait — you came home?" I asked. I hadn't even noticed.

"Yeah. Not for long. I ducked into the kitchen and back out again. You wouldn't have seen me."

"Here," I said, handing her phone to her.

"What do I do?" she asked quietly, absently rubbing the screen clean with the hem of her shirt. "What do I tell Mom and Dad?"

I felt even more sick. "This is a hell of a lot more serious than getting in trouble with Mom and Dad! Maya. You could go to jail. You could spend your *whole life in prison*."

"No, I can't. Because I didn't kill him."

"That's sort of irrelevant, right? It looks like you did, and that's what matters."

"But you believe me. Tell me you believe me," she begged.

"Sure," I said, but I knew I didn't sound convincing.

"There'll be an investigation, right? And they'll figure out the truth?"

"You're not even sure what the truth *is*. You're just 'pretty sure' you didn't kill him. The police aren't going to buy that. It's not nearly good enough."

"I can't believe you don't believe me!"

I sighed. Why wasn't she getting it? "I'm trying to keep you safe. Don't start doubting me. I'm the one definite ally you've got in all this, you know that?"

She let out a long, guttering breath, pressed her face into the wall. "I'm sorry. I know that. . . . I'm going to have to lean on you from here on out. Can I lean on you, like I used to?"

She'd never acknowledged that her behavior had ever caused me any burden whatsoever. It was amazing, how much pity I had for her at that moment, even in that terrible circumstance. I hugged her again. This time I wasn't smelling evidence on her clothes. I was just pressing her tight. And at the same time, I knew I was being played. Maya still believed she could flirt her way out of anything, even murder.

"What," I said eventually, "are we going to do about his car?"

"What do you mean?" Maya asked.

"You took his car."

"*I took his car?!* Where is it?" She crushed her hands against the sides of her head. "What the hell is wrong with me?" she wailed. "How can I not remember taking his *car*? I swear I didn't. I saw it — someone else was driving it. I think. I mean, if you say I did, I probably did, but I really don't think I did."

"Well, it's right down the block, farther down Langdell. We can't leave it here. They'll trace it to you."

"No, they won't. I didn't touch it. So what if his car's parked downtown, sorta near a tattoo parlor I go to sometimes? How does that trace back to me?"

She was right, when I thought about it. But I still wanted to get everything related to Jefferson as far away as possible. "Did you leave anything in the car?" I asked.

She frowned. "I don't think so. I swear I didn't move that car."

I sighed. "Cheyenne and I'll take a look."

"What do I do with myself?" Maya asked. "I don't know where to go."

"Look," I said, "you can't go to Mom and Dad. You can't put them in that position, and regardless, you might not like what they decide to do about it. You're going to have to stop using your cell phone and e-mail and everything else. Those can all be traced."

"Grandma Veronica. I'll go stay with Veronica."

"If you're missing, you know they're going to check her house."

"You sure? She's just our one-time stepmother's mom. Okay, yeah, maybe, eventually they'll come to her place. She'll find another place to hide me by then. I trust her, Abby. She's the only person in this world I trust, except for you."

I had no doubt Maya would add more names to this list as soon as it became convenient. "Fine," I said. "You have to go there immediately. I don't know how I'm going to drop you off at the same time as checking Jefferson's car and —"

"Abby, calm down. I'll take a bus. I know how to take a bus."

"No, we'll drop you off. It's okay."

"Abby . . ."

"Don't ask me for anything. This is the last time I bail you out, do you understand?" I said, my temper flaring. "You have no idea what a mess you're putting our whole family in. I'm terrified, I'm sick, I'm —"

"I just need you to get my jeans from upstairs."

"Oh. Fine. I'll go get your flipping jeans."

She knew exactly how to play me, as always. As soon as I started to get angry, she'd direct me toward practical things. She played helpless, got me concentrating on lost denim long enough for me to stop thinking about lost sisterhood. It had always worked.

7.

Maya tried to chicken out and wait at the parking lot, but I told her she had to come with us, since seeing Jefferson's car might jog her memory.

We stood around the driver's side window. Cody, perplexed and tired, sulked in the dirt.

"Where did you put the keys?" I asked Maya.

"I swear, I never had any keys."

"You got this car here somehow, sweetheart," Cheyenne said, rolling her eyes.

"I don't *know*," Maya wailed. "I really, really don't!"

"Okay, shh, keep *quiet*," I said.

If downtown hadn't been so totally deserted, we wouldn't have had the nerve to stand there staring into a dead boy's car. Even so, I kept scanning around to see if we were being watched. Except for one homeless guy who was far more concerned with collecting soda bottles from a trash heap, we were alone.

A collection of Mardi Gras beads dangled from the rearview mirror, one sun-silvered purple length snarled around a Xavier High School parking pass. A fast-food cup was wedged next to the parking brake, its plastic lid half off, a small pile of ash around the straw hole. Jefferson's messenger bag was on the passenger-side floor, the flap open to reveal a neat block of textbooks. A sweatshirt had been thrown in back. The driver's seat was draped with one of those cab driver beaded covers. A glass pipe nestled in the ashtray. Faded parking passes from the clubbing district curled under the windshield.

"Maya," Cheyenne said, "isn't that your sweatshirt?"

"Where?"

"On the backseat."

"I don't — shit shit shit," she said.

"We have to get in there," I said. "You need to think. Where are the keys? You must remember having them in your hands at some point. Don't you remember putting them somewhere? In a pocket?"

"I don't have pockets," Maya said. "And I don't remember any keys. I don't remember *driving*."

"It's amazing you're alive," Cheyenne said. "That you're not wrapped around a tree somewhere."

I put my hand on Cheyenne's arm to stop her — if Maya withdrew any more we'd never get her back. "I'll call Keith later and see what he might know," I said. "In the meantime, we need to get you out of here."

I knew that once the police started looking for Maya, they'd eventually get to Veronica's house. The police could be on top of us at any moment. But what choice did we have, really? Veronica's was the best of a short list of options.

The ride to Grandma Veronica's house: Cheyenne at the wheel, me in shotgun, Maya slouching out of view in back, like a politician tipped off to an assassination plot. No one said anything. The only sound was Maya slurping her slushie, which she'd insisted we stop and buy her. She was living deep in her mind, silent and preoccupied. I imagined her replaying last night over and over in her head, trying to determine what the truth really was. The whole vibe felt like our family trips during the divorce year.

Veronica lived by herself half an hour out of town, in a creaky suburban development centered on a communal pool clogged with pine needles and toddler poo. By all rights, Maya and I should have hated her: She was the mother of the woman who split up our mom and dad, after all. But that office affair ended after a year, and Dad went back to Mom. No one was in touch with the "adulterous whore" (Mom's words, clearly), but Maya and I couldn't quite give up Veronica. She was a little crass and loud, sure. Crazy hair — white and fluffy as a dandelion, with one store-dyed huge brown streak — and really fun. Independent, even though she was in her seventies. She would buy a truckload of art supplies each Sunday and spend the week making T-shirts and selling them online. She actually made a living out of it, when you added in Social Security payments.

Cheyenne took the curves of Veronica's subdivision at high speed, making the fillings in my molars rattle. Normally, parking under Veronica's carport involves a quiet crunching sound of fronds and clippings and dead insects going under the tires, but today there was a roar and a whump as Cheyenne slammed the cement block at the head of the parking spot. Cody growled.

"Hey, cool it," I said. "You're not making us look totally suspicious or anything."

Maya peered up and down the subdivision before she got out of the car, like there might have been SWAT teams on the roof waiting for the chance to sight their rifles on her. Cheyenne and I shuttled her to Veronica's door. I opened Veronica's gate and shooed Cody out back before we rang the doorbell.

Veronica opened the door, holding a tabby and shaking her foot at a calico trying to escape. Other cats howled farther in the house. "Girls! Come in. Oh, shit."

The calico got out. I leaped for him, but it was Cheyenne who stopped him . . . by stepping on his tail. He howled. "Thanks a lot," Veronica said in a curious tone, like she wanted to drop-kick Cheyenne as much as thank her.

As soon as we were over the threshold and the door had closed, Maya sank to the shag carpet. "Oh, thank god," she murmured into the nylon fibers.

Veronica stopped in the middle of her autopilot trip to the coffeepot and placed her hands on her hips. "What the hell is going on, ladies?"

Maya peered at me from the floor, tears filling her eyes. "I can't do this right now. Abby, you tell her."

Veronica resumed her trip to the coffee machine. "I'll make a full pot, I think. Cheyenne, I know efficient girls like you adore coffee."

"We don't have time," I said.

I started by telling Veronica about Jefferson's messing around on Maya, then moved on to Maya coming to find him and getting worked up, the strike on his head, the fall he must have taken into the river as he staggered. Veronica listened intently.

"You didn't kill him," was the first thing she said once I was finished. She placed her healing hands on Maya, who had lain on the couch and pulled a corduroy backrest over her face.

"I hit him really hard," Maya said. "He was bleeding. And he's dead now. It doesn't feel good at all."

With me Maya was defensive, but to Veronica she was all but confessing. I felt a shiver of jealousy at their closeness. Veronica went to the couch, pulled the backrest away, and sat down next to Maya, gathering her in her arms. "Shh. Of course you didn't. He deserved to be hit, honey. He was scum."

Cheyenne, left standing next to me at the counter, arched an eyebrow: *Is this going to become the official history, that Jefferson deserved to die?*

"We have to figure out what to do with Maya," I said, wishing I was part of that broth of compassion on the couch. I displayed my hand on the table, palm up, the way people in couples do when they want to be held.

Cheyenne didn't notice. "I don't think she should go back to your parents," she said.

"Absolutely not," Veronica said. "It would put your father in an impossible position. She'll stay here." She hugged Maya closer. "Won't you, darling?"

"If Maya's missing, the police will come here," Cheyenne said flatly. "I don't think it's a good idea."

"You're totally right," I said. "But what other choice do we have for now? No one's got cash for a hotel. We'll move her as soon as we can. Once we know who the police are gunning for, we can decide whether Maya should come out of hiding. If they're on the hunt for her, then we'll move her someplace. This is our best option until then."

"If I'm in hiding," Maya sniffed, "it just looks even more like I killed him."

"If you're *not* in hiding," I said, "then you're in police custody. You can tell them you're innocent as much as you want, but I'm sorry, they won't believe you."

Maya began to shake. Veronica gripped her tighter. "Shh, honey, shh. Abby, really! Watch what you're saying!"

"What?" I yelled. I'd been calm until then, but apparently I'd been simmering beneath; I was surprised by my own rage. "Are you mad at me because I'm being *harsh*? I'm doing my best to give Maya the benefit of the doubt. If she's guilty, we're all accomplices here. Even Cheyenne, who has no reason at all to stick her head out yet again for my screwed-up sister. It's not her fault that Maya's become nasty and self-centered, and then went and maybe *killed* someone. I know you say you didn't do it, Maya — but it's not looking real good right now."

"Abby," Cheyenne said, finally taking my hand. "Keep your voice down, okay?"

"I am *not* nasty," Maya said, typically choosing the most minor point to fixate on.

"This is ridiculous," I said. "I don't know why I'm sticking around and trying to help you."

Something clicked in Maya: the horror of her situation, the very small number of people she could call allies, or maybe the contortions I was going through to keep her away from the police. She got up from the couch and stood next to me, almost took my hand. "Abby," she said, "I know you could have turned me in. But you didn't. I swear I didn't kill Jefferson. I *swear* it. Since you're helping me, I think somewhere deep down you must believe me. I need you. I've always needed you, but now more than ever. Please don't give up on me now."

I was in shock. My anger sputtered away. That's how it had always been: I needed so little encouragement to pledge myself to her.

"Look, Maya," I said. "I know you'd never mean to kill someone. And I do find it hard to believe you killed Jefferson. If you didn't, someone did. And until we find out who that is, you're going to be the number one suspect."

"I know," she whispered. "I get that."

We hung there for a second. I felt such a strange closeness

to her. It was as if I'd been waiting until this moment to realize: We were in this together.

"Why don't you go take a nap?" Veronica suggested to Maya. She was more than willing to oblige, lumbering away with eyes half closed. Once she'd left earshot, Veronica turned to me and Cheyenne and said, "She can't stay here. I'd love to take care of her, but the police will be on my place in no time. I'm going to find her someplace safe to stay."

"You'll tell me where it is as soon as you do?" I asked.

Veronica nodded. "Of course. The official story, though, is that you have no idea where she is. I'm not going to tell you the exact location, so you have less to hide from the police. And I don't want any talk about whether she actually did it, do you hear me? She's innocent, end of story."

"What do I tell my parents?" I asked.

"You haven't seen Maya in days," Veronica said flatly. "Done."

"I don't know if I can pull it off," I said, though I was pretty sure I could. Lying to my parents had never been too hard. They never expected it from me.

"I don't think you two are considering," Cheyenne said, "the most obvious option. Maya should turn herself in. She can say she didn't do it, but that she hit Jefferson and she's worried because she hasn't heard from him since last night. Come clean."

Veronica glanced at Cheyenne dismissively. "You're a

smart girl, Cheyenne, but no. The minute the police get their hands on Maya, she'll tell them anything they want to hear. She's scared and easily steered into a dead end. Right now, Maya is just missing. It's possible the police will think she and Jefferson were both attacked by some stranger, that Jefferson defended them, that Maya either escaped or was kidnapped. She shouldn't go and disprove that."

"But if we go ahead with your plan," I said, my stomach clenching even harder than it had all day, "my parents will start to worry that Maya's dead. We can't do that to them."

"We have to," Veronica said. "I'm sorry, but I'm not letting my Maya get anywhere near a police station. I wouldn't put her in that position for anything."

"In the meantime," I whispered dully, "I'll just watch my family fall apart as I search for the real killer."

"I'm here to help," Cheyenne said. "You won't be alone."

"Don't search for anyone," Veronica said. "Don't draw any attention to us. Sounds like not many people knew about Maya and Jefferson's relationship — it might take the police a long time to make the connection. Keep your whole family off their radar, okay?" She reached a hand into a homemade pottery vase by the front door and pulled out a quarter. She pressed it into my hand, then apparently thought better of it and pressed it into Cheyenne's instead.

"What's this?" Cheyenne asked.

"You're finding a pay phone that's at least a few miles away and making a call," Veronica said. "An anonymous tip that there's a body to be found. It's time that that poor boy's parents found out. And after that, neither of you are to bring up Jefferson Andrews, ever again. And remember, Maya's dead to you."

I thought it a strange choice of words, given the circumstances. But I didn't question them. For all I knew, Veronica was having us hide Maya from the police because she thought she really did it.

I ducked into the spare bedroom to say my good-bye to Maya.

I had no idea when I'd see her again.

But we didn't admit that to each other. We didn't hug, didn't make it a big deal.

We just let each other go to wherever life was about to drag us.

I sat in the idling car in the mall parking lot, watching as Cheyenne used the pay phone. A bunch of freshmen boys from our school passed by, pushing one another. I slinked out of view as they passed.

Cheyenne finished the call, dashed over, landed heavily into the seat, and put the car in gear.

"All done?" I asked.

"All done."

Jefferson's death was now officially revealed. Police would be driving to the ravine, sirens blaring.

There was no going back now.

8.

Cheyenne wanted to come inside my house with me, but I knew pretending not to know where Maya was would be hard enough without Cheyenne around to complicate things. So I said good-bye and walked up the driveway alone.

Our front yard was an eternal source of neighborhood snickering. For one thing, you couldn't see a square foot of free driveway. The garage was jammed by a pair of antique cars that my dad had been trying to get running forever — we had baby pictures of Maya bouncing on the seats, and they hadn't moved before or since. Because the garage was filled with cars that didn't move, all the rest of our crap was in the driveway, in full view of the rest of the neighborhood. There was my car, an old white clunker that came with a sticker in the back window of a boy peeing on a Chevy sign that I'd only half managed to scratch off, a riding mower, and my parents' cars, a matching pair of BMWs. They each had vanity plates, MOM'S BEAMER and DAD'S BEAMER. But they were nothing compared to the boat, a glittering hunk of plastic that looked like a way oversize Christmas ornament. We hadn't gone sailing in years. We didn't even own a truck anymore, so we couldn't budge it. The only use it'd had in the last decade was when the neighbor's cat gave birth to seven kittens underneath it. But we had the boat status symbol, which cast a shadow on the house and the whole neighborhood.

If the outside of the house was pure excess, the inside was pure constraint. As I unlocked the door and pushed it open, calling out to see if my mother was home, my voice rang out down the drab ("Roman tile") hallway and the empty ("minimalist!") living room, through the cruel ("Bessemer steel appliances!") kitchen. I'd never been a fan of our house — there was nothing on the walls because the plaster couldn't be marred; our couches didn't have cushions so that the lines were clean — but its fashionableness was a huge source of pride for my mom. She looked forward to polishing the silver every Sunday morning as much as the other moms in our subdivision anticipated facials. Who was I to complain about her getting happy, even if by the shallowest methods? Her interior design drugs were much cheaper than Maya's chemical ones.

Luckily, my parents were out running errands when I returned from spiriting Maya away. Cody bounded to the laundry room, started slurping up water. Poor girl. I shut the dog gate. She was allowed in the laundry room or out back, but no dog hair anywhere else in the house.

One good thing about Maya choosing to live in the basement was that I got both of the upstairs bedrooms and the bathroom joining them. I closed the doors and put some music on high. Its thick, powerful twang calmed and strengthened me. I knew that I didn't have any time to waste. I had to spin this story the right way, and that would mean steering everyone in the correct directions right from the beginning.

I started the shower running, stripped, and stared at myself in the mirror. Still the same naked Abby, red elbows and pale freckled thighs.

The backs of my arms were already dried out from the extra-long shower I'd taken the night before, but I had to clean again. I put the water on its hottest setting, until steam was truly billowing from the bathroom. I gasped, then gave in to the distraction of the pain and pleasure.

Once I'd showered and dressed in comfortable, clean T-shirt and sweats, I turned the music up even louder and lay on my bed. I'd allow myself one sweet minute of rest.

First step, I reasoned, was to finally take a good look at what was in Maya's basement, see if there was anything down there that might incriminate her. Should I wear gloves? No — no one would care if my fingerprints were in my own house. As I went down the stairs, I leaned on the handrails so they wouldn't creak. I knew there was no chance of Maya barging in, but she always made such a big deal about her personal space that I was nervous, anyway.

She had placed black paper cones over the basement's overhead lamps, so the floor was dark except where it was broken by stray shafts of light. Only the barest illumination hit the paraphernalia of Maya's life — and everything she owned was best called paraphernalia. Remnants of cut-up magazines, tubes of paints and makeup, curled and dusty posters of cute boys back from the days of her more knowable preteen existence, bumper stickers for bands with too many consonants in their names, a curling guitar she once found along the side of the road and took home, even though the wood was warping, the frets rimmed green with fungus. Some of the sweet sister who used to lean against me at the school bus stop remained — propped up between an eight ball and a cracked lava lamp was a crayon portrayal of an airport, done with a nine-year-old's sense of perspective, planes crammed one on top of the next, crossing impossible dimensions as Maya tried to figure out how to make them all fit on the page. Wigs, some normal and some crazy and pink. She loved to go out looking like she wasn't her.

No one else had come in here for months, not even my mother. Maya was all about setting up these airtight boundaries: no sunlight on her white skin; no sharing a toothpaste tube with anyone, least of all me; no talking about her feelings or what was always making her so sullen. I felt a sense of weird unholiness, like I'd entered some foreign church. I ran my fingers over the keys of an old typewriter, flipped through a graphic novel. Four of them were on Maya's bed, on and under the velvety sheets, testaments to how long ago it'd been since she'd actually slept at home and needed to use her bed as anything but storage.

At the foot of the bed, slotted in between a selection of paperbacks and a few random volumes of *The Book of Knowledge* filched from the den upstairs — *T, PQ, A* — was a book with a plain binding. I pulled it down and opened it with one finger.

There were drawings on the first few pages, clumsy, vivid, and energetic. The crosshatching of a black moth's wings indented the paper ten pages farther in. Then the journaling began.

...not sure whether I don't like them and so I don't like being with them, or if I just don't relate to them and so I decide I don't like them, just so I'll never know they never liked me, that's a fun circle, huh?!...

...present myself fully so that no one will ask any questions...

...I doing? He's so not my type...

...stand her. How is it possible that we were both raised by the same parents? But they're just like her. Conformist. Middle class. Boring. I'm the one who was pushed into the nest by a cuckoo bird or something. Tried to ask her last night how she really felt about the fact that he wasn't talking to her anymore. It's a total teenage thing, right, to get upset about some guy not liking you back, so I expected her to say something, but she just shut down totally. Or turned it on totally is more like it. Got real chirpy. I'm like, really? Why are you <u>smiling?</u> This rejection's got you <u>thrilled?</u> It's not like she's fake. It's that she's not fully real. Where's the suffering? She can't really be as happy as she lets on. But what the hell, everyone likes her and she got into Vanderbilt and

my parents probably wish they'd stopped having kids after her so maybe that's the key after all, everyone thinks your golden or everyone thinks your shit. (me included? What do I think of me?) Huh. Tougher one is how does she feel about her? ...

...totally hot. I don't care what they think. They don't know how I scream. And I can't describe it, even to my best friends, without sounding like a total slut....

...he's really sweet. I just wish I liked him more. When I touch him, it's like his body moves more than I'd expect it to....

...like I was finally really present in the world. We dunked underwater, and it was like we could have stayed down there for an hour if we wanted. But we didn't want to, I guess. I thought I did. When I came up my heart was thumping so hard it was like a dance beat. At the time I was sure he heard it and that that was what we danced to. But you know what, I was high, and I'm just going to have to figure out that those things I think are huge truths while youre high are just you being you and wishing others were you as well....

I flipped to the last page. It was dated a few months ago. A playlist for a mix CD, lots of crossouts and scribbling.

She thought I was fake, huh? Because what, I tried at school, because I didn't drop out and stop talking to my family, just to end up throwing my tits at the GED tutor my parents paid good money to have come to the house twice a week? It's like she thought the only way to be real was never to do what was expected. I sort of got why some kids went really goth and started driving hundreds of miles to go to renaissance fairs or hardcore concerts or whatever, but Maya was like one of those pseudo-emo kids who buy black lipstick and get a belly button piercing just because she knows teachers will go tsk-tsk and her parents will freak. Pissing people off and saying you're all unique isn't enough. Actually becoming unique would be something. Maya made being disappointed a lifestyle. No wonder everyone found it impossible to spend time with her, even her own parents.

Really, it was no wonder Maya detested me.

Yes, she detested me. But I was the one who had her future in my hands.

I pulled back the sheets. Nothing was there, beyond a musty smell.

I dug into the room, pulling open drawers, tossing around laundry, lifting the mattress and peering underneath. I didn't find anything but receipts and notes that would take hours to go through. I'd save that task for when I got more desperate. Unable to stop myself, I made Maya's bed. I couldn't stand the idea of it looking like a disaster if the police came to investigate.

As I was straightening Maya's sheets, I swept the random encyclopedias to the floor. Shreds of paper fell out of *T*. I opened the volume and saw that Maya had gone after the inside pages with an X-Acto knife. Classic trick — book as secret storage. She seemed to have botched *T*, though — the insides looked like a used piñata. I opened *PQ*, and then *A* — Aha. Inside was a plastic-wrapped bundle of some-thing soft and brown, moist like sod. I recognized a drug, even if I had no idea which one it was. A note on top, in tight, controlled handwriting I knew to be Jefferson's: *30 Langdell, #4D.* I memorized the address, replaced the note, and shoved the book deep under her bed. There was a rum-ble from the driveway.

My parents were home.

9.

Before the front door had even closed, my dad called out, "Family meeting!" Almost instantly, I could hear my mom getting out the club soda, a drink she thought lent formality and which always signified something major was happening. Family meetings were the only times anyone but my father used the den, and I'd never known oak and dusty brass to be so intimidating. His den was a dark, meticulously organized place, and to me it screamed "divorce, divorce, divorce," probably because four years ago, during our most memorable family meeting ever, *divorce* was the only word Maya and I heard.

I walked in, said, "What's up?" and watched my mom slide ice cubes into a glass and pour me some popping water. I'm often struck by how pretty she is. She has this muscle-plump body and amazing red hair that's so full and lovely it looks like a wig, and in that way actually does her a disservice. She wears pearls a lot, but so naturally that they look casual. She's always focusing on other people. I'll be happy to be like her when I'm that age.

"Where," my dad said, "is your sister?"

"I don't know," I said, looking between my dad and mom and back again. "Why?"

"We're worried," my dad said. "I might as well just tell

you and get it over with." He paused, like he was taking a deep breath, but his chest was still. "Your mother got a phone call from Gail's mother. It appears that Maya's tutor, Jefferson, is dead."

"Andrews?" Like there was more than one Jefferson tutoring Maya. Like I hadn't been living for hours with the reality of what he'd just told me.

Mom nodded. Dad leaned against the bar and looked at me. He's like that — he'll move away from you when he's most concerned, as if to give you extra space in which to soak in his compassion.

"He's dead?" I squeaked.

"Yes," Mom said. "And we want to know where Maya is. It's very important, honey."

"Did you know him well? Was he a friend?" Dad asked.

I shrugged. "He was Maya's tutor. Big man around school, too. Hard to miss him. Oh god. This is for real, huh?"

"I'm sorry, honey," Mom said.

I knew this had to be a perfect performance, that I had to be careful not to overdo it. But a strange thing happened — hearing the news coming from them was almost as surreal as learning it the first time. Even though they weren't telling me anything new, the fact that we were having this conversation still shook me. And that helped make my lying more convincing.

"How did he die?" I asked.

"Apparently, the police located him at the bottom of a ravine," Mom said.

"What was he doing at the bottom of a ravine?" I asked.

"Drowned," Dad said. "Or maybe hit his head. Someone called in a tip — that's the only reason they knew there was a body to be found at all. Simon Lawrence — Gail's dad — is on the police force, so he had some of the — details. It was an accident, probably. Did he seem unhappy or withdrawn recently?"

"No," I said. "Why would someone call in an anonymous tip? Doesn't that make whoever it was the killer?"

"Tips aren't always anonymous, Abby," Dad said. "Though I can see how you'd just assume so. This one happened to be, yes. It's probably from someone who didn't want to get entangled in a police investigation. I can't say I entirely blame her."

"Her?" my mother said sharply, tension setting the silk of her shirt to fluttering. "You didn't tell me it was a woman. It couldn't be Maya who called it in, could it?"

"Margot, please," my father said.

"Don't. You can't say that I'm being ridiculous. We haven't seen her in days, and she's not answering her phone." Her fingers flicked against one another, finally occupying themselves running up and down her pearls like a rosary.

"I'm sure she's not involved," Dad said, looking right through me.

"Of course not," I said. I clasped my mom's hand. I couldn't quite bring myself to look at my dad. I'd always been intimidated by him. Desperate to please him, too, but scared. He seemed invulnerable, a mover. He did things in the world, while I always had to resort to the strategies of the weak: sulking and pleading. Caring. I knew if he kept staring at me he'd see the truth in my eyes and act on it, start flipping out. All I wanted was for everyone to stay as calm as possible. I needed time.

"If you learn anything, Abby, you'll inform us right away," Dad said. He stared at me with that penetrating look of his, handsome features overwhelmed by broad cheeks and rolls of wet black curls.

"The days of Maya leaning on me are long gone," I told him. "I don't think you can count on her reaching out."

If my parents were feeling any pangs of regret at not having kept their younger daughter nearer to them, they had gotten used to them long ago. They really had done everything they could to help Maya. They'd tried being super-strict. They'd tried being super-lenient. They'd sent her to a small horde of therapists, tidy beige PhD business cards cramming an envelope in the hardware drawer. Finally, the only way for my parents to keep her in their lives at all had been to give her a long leash. If they didn't complain when she only came home every other day, she wouldn't punish them by hiding herself away for two weeks straight.

"Guess we'll have to find her another tutor," I said.

My parents stared at me. "Abby, that's not funny in the least," my mother said.

I let some of the tears I'd been holding back release. "I know. I feel so weird. I think I'm in shock. Jefferson can't really be dead."

"Oh, sweetheart," Mom said, hugging me.

My father downed his soda. "I can't even imagine what the Andrewses are going through."

"I can," Mom said. And she left it at that.

10.

Word traveled fast. I didn't have to work hard to find out what people were saying, not when everyone was posting their thoughts online. I started with Gail Lawrence, since her dad had been my parents' first source of information. There it was, at the top of her page: Jefferson Andrews, RIP. You'll keep living in our hearts.

There was ten minutes of online silence, and then the other posts started. So many questions. So much feeling. None of it really mattering, because the person it was all directed at was gone.

I clicked on Jefferson's page and that's when it first hit me that someone's death could feel so real and yet unreal, so final and yet imaginary. Online, Jefferson was frozen forever in the evening before he died. If he could have predicted he was going to be killed, what would he have chosen for his final posting? Surely not Jefferson is going to ride it hard tonight, left Friday at 6:15 P.M.

In the comments section, one of his friends had posted, nonsensically, Yeah, Rose is going 2 B saying on Monday, man?, followed by poser comments by some other guys, predictably going for the most obvious innuendos. The commenting carried on through Friday night — none of them knew that he was dead, that even as they were goading his sexploits, he was bleeding into the dark river, thunderstorms pummeling his corpse.

The first sign that something had gone wrong appeared at two A.M. From Rose: J, baby, thought you were supposed to come by my house. Chk voice mail!!!

Then, again from Rose, at 3:23 A.M.: Dont bother calling. Anyone reading this let him know hes n major trouble.

Around four A.M.: nvm he's not worth it. Tell him that instead.

Trailing after their queen, the various handmaidens in their various degrees of love with Jefferson started their various postings. They, too, had gone too long without the fix of his sporadic contact. Rachael McHenry posted hey buddy some psycho girl got you hidden away? as if she herself hadn't turned psycho on him last winter.

After the news of his death got out, the comments turned to testimonials, got weepy and overwrought. Cara Johnson wrote from her boarding school, where she'd been sent after carving up her arm post-breakup: If you're dead then we should all be dead. Ill switch places with you!!! Some others, like from Jefferson's guy friends, were spare: will miss you, bud. One of the super-religious kids called him a holy light called up to guide the walkways of heaven. Most of the posts were addressed directly to Jefferson, saying how missed he would be and how tragically short his time on Earth had been. One wished him the best of luck in his next life. I found it all really weird, like our accounts were heaven year-books, like there was angel wi-fi.

The worst:

My Darling Jefferson,

It's 7:47 pm, almost three hours since they found your body. They say your heart stopped but I think it was just too large for all the love that you held. Unconditional Love is the most powerful emotion there is and You Are Its Prince. The one and only Prince of Xavier High.

Posted by Jenna Michaelson, an exchange student Jefferson always made fun of for having fat lips.

The trail leading from the present moment back in time to Jefferson's murder was here, catalogued on some distant server. Since I couldn't glean anything more from the recent comments, I went back in time to when Jefferson was alive. Rose's words appeared everywhere on his page, of course, alongside carefully selected photos of the two of them where she looked hot and Jefferson looked in love. I wondered about the ones she hadn't uploaded, the ones where he was distracted and looking off camera for his next seduction.

There was a roster of regular posters. Tons of comments were from the three girls everyone knew Jefferson had messed around with: Cara, Rachael, and Donna. But there were some unexpected posts, too, like Go straight to H's. Blake is watching from none other than tattoo parlor Keith.

Who was Blake? I wrote down the name on the back of my planner.

Then, far into the past from Jefferson's front page, I found a post from Cheyenne: I'm back now. Call me about it if you're still up. What was she doing messaging him? The "it" she referred to was probably homework . . . but still, she always said how much she hated him. A late-night posting seemed odd.

I clicked through his page, back and back until I was witnessing his life months in the past. I couldn't stop; I wanted to live forever in that period when he'd been alive, when the world had been ordinary and even boring. If I could go back then, knowing what I knew now, I would write to him: Be good to the ones who adore you. Because, as it turns out, one of them may kill you.

I kept telling myself that each page would be the last. But I continued searching. I realized that I was looking for someone. Not as my main purpose, but as a side curiosity. Caitlin, the girl that Maya had mentioned. Caitlin, who Jefferson said had a nice ass.

Nowhere. Not a mention.

Finally, I surfed away from Jefferson's page and on to Maya's. It seemed she'd obeyed me and hadn't gone online since I'd talked to her, thank god.

Her last update had come from her phone, eleven P.M. last night, probably right after Jefferson had died.

I'm lost.

MONDAY, MAY 13

11.

I spent Sunday worrying about Maya and accomplishing nothing, and it wasn't until the evening that it hit me that I would have to go to school the next day. Could I pretend to act normal, could I possibly concentrate on schoolwork and APs and graduation plans? How would I answer everyone's questions? By early Monday morning, my plan had switched to dodging school entirely. I couldn't take all the group pomp that was bound to happen. If it was anything like what had happened after those boys almost decapitated one another in that sword incident last year, there would be a somber message on the morning announcements, and then the whole school would crack open. There'd be an assembly and maybe shrinks brought in to stop us from throwing ourselves in front of trucks. Everyone would be concerned and caring and suspicious and awful. They'd ask me what I knew and I'd mess up my answer. Maybe a big plug would come undone at the base of my skull and all this steaming gray truth would come boiling out. I didn't know what was going to happen, and that was why I couldn't let it start.

I'd tried to call Veronica a few times on Sunday, but she never picked up. It was for the best that she avoided outside contact, but it still had me worried not to know what was going on with Maya. I showered like usual, picked up the lunch my mom left for me, weathered a squeamishly long hug, got into my car, and headed in the direction of school. But I chose the right turn lane when I technically should have gone left, and any possibility of Monday being a school day was history. I traveled the couple of exits to Veronica's. Cheyenne called while I was on the way, undoubtedly because she'd seen I wasn't at school and wanted to make sure I was okay. I let her go to voice mail — I'd never done that to her before.

Veronica answered the door in a sari she'd bought in a thrift store years ago and wore on days when she said she was working but was actually watching talk shows. Her hair was in curlers. Who actually wore curlers in the twenty-first century?

"What are you doing here, honey?" she asked.

"I wanted to check on Maya. How's she doing?"

"Come in," Veronica said.

"She's not here anymore, huh?" I said as she sat me on the couch.

"How do you know me so well?" Veronica said. She had this sigh in her voice, like she was expecting me to fight. So I did.

"Don't try to soften this," I said. "You're supposed to be taking care of her."

"I know I am, Abby," she snapped. "And watch your tone. I'm not your little sister. I won't have you muscling me around."

"So where is she?" I asked.

"You need to be involved as little as possible," she said. "I say that for your protection. The less you know about where she is, the better off you are. Rest assured that I've sent Maya to a secure place. The police won't find her."

"This is not the plan, Vee. You promised to tell me where you sent her. Is she around here? Is she still even in *Florida*?"

"You know I'm not going to tell you anything more. Do you want an oatmeal cookie? Made them this morning."

"I know you mean well, but it's not a good idea. I'm eighteen. I can handle whatever's coming. You're not about to start cutting me out of the loop."

"It's not a question of whether you can handle it. I have no doubt you're capable enough, darling. It's whether you *should*. Assisting in anything illegal is very serious. I'm at a stage of life where I'm willing to take on the risk. Even if you think you are, you're too young to make an informed decision. This really isn't up for discussion."

It was like the air pressure in the room was increasing. I could feel my mind getting heavier — Veronica going rogue could jeopardize everything, but I couldn't figure out how to stop her. "I'm her sister. I know you're close to Maya, but you're not even related to her."

"Abby, you should be in school. It's not a good idea for you to even be here. It looks suspicious. Go back. Find out what you can. We need to clear Maya's name, if we can. And for that we need information."

"You're not going to tell me anything, are you?"

She agitatedly picked up an artsy nudes book from the coffee table and put it back down. "Goddammit. Look, Maya doesn't *want* you to know."

"She doesn't want me to know where she is? She wants to get away from me, is that what you're trying to tell me? Even after I saved her ass?"

"She's hysterical. She wants to live on her own terms for a while. It makes sense to me. Give her some space. Let me take care of her. You take care of yourself, Abby."

Unbelievable.

Veronica was one of the few people who used people's names when talking to them, like in a soap opera. She was a woman with . . . flair. *A highly developed sense of the dramatic*, my mom had once called it, not kindly. Who knew what crazy plan Veronica had concocted with Maya — neither of them was exactly stable. Suddenly, I was on my feet, hurling open doors. The first led to Veronica's bedroom, tassled bedspread neatly made, romance novels on the bedstand. The next to a toilet, seashell soaps. The next to the laundry room.

"Abby! Excuse me! Abigail Goodwin! What do you think you're doing?"

She didn't dare try to stop me, though. Eventually, I got to the last possible door, at the back of the hallway. It was locked. "What's in here?" I demanded.

"There's no way I'm going to answer a question thrown in my face like that. Get over it, Abby. Maya isn't here."

84

Already the energy was seeping out of me. I knew I'd been acting extreme. "Why won't you open the door, then?"

"Because I've chosen to keep it locked. That's my right. It's not your right to know, Abby." On the last "Abby," she took my hand. "Your feelings are hurt, aren't they, honey?" she said. "You want to be the protective big sister. I get it."

She wasn't describing exactly what I was feeling. But it was true that I'd spent so long being the big sister that I didn't know any other way to be around Maya (or so Cheyenne always phrased it); Veronica had hit close enough to home, and she'd offered warm empathy when I least expected it. If I didn't catch myself, pretty soon I'd be gushing tears.

Veronica mopped my face with a tea towel, as if I actually had cried. I headed toward the front door. Veronica loved me but also wanted me out of there, I knew.

"Abby," Veronica said as I stood by the door, "what I'm about to say is for your safety as much as Maya's."

"What?"

"Don't come here anymore. Not until I tell you it's okay."

I hugged her before I left. My hand pressed the tea towel draped over her shoulder. It was wet; I guess I had cried after all.

12.

I realized as I was leaving Veronica's that I'd been dumb to think it was a good idea to skip school — wouldn't a classmate's dying make most people crave company, comfort, gossip, and confirmation? Missing school sent the message that I was either unfeeling or very deeply upset, for some specific reason. It would look suspicious for me not to show. So what if I was feeling moody and weird. Everyone else would be, too, right?

I'd predicted the assembly would be awful, and I was right. Bleachers full of slumping teenagers with tearstained faces, a couple of cops, and some people in polo shirts with briefcases — probably shrinks. Lots and lots of bawling kids. Jefferson's closest friends, five guys best described as bros, shoulder to shoulder, hands shielding their eyes, bodies clustered but not touching, surrounded on either side by long blank spaces of orange bleacher. Pimply loners looking paler than usual. Some sophomore chicks who wouldn't have gotten the time of day from Jefferson, absolutely hysterical with tears. Teachers, white-knuckled and serious, holding hands like there'd been a school shooting. Our principal gave a warbly speech, trying to project confidence but really just a wreck, clearly unequipped for anything like this.

I was seated in back beside Cheyenne and a couple other friends. Their calculus quiz had been cut short by the assembly, and while the principal spoke, Sandra and Martine were discussing whether integrating trig functions would be on the final. The rest of my friends were scattered throughout the gymnasium, springing up in the background everywhere I looked. Even though they were right in front of me, I missed them immensely. I hadn't spoken to them all weekend and couldn't imagine what I would say now. I found myself wondering, for the first time, whether I really knew any of them. Were *they* capable of murder? Of course not. Any of the stupid fights we'd ever had seemed like charming kids' stories. Would they still feel they could tell me their troubles, given the weightiness of mine? I couldn't bring myself to find out. Their voice mails had been mounting up on my phone. One waved across the gymnasium, and I shot back a look of broad, unspecific concern.

The principal was still carrying on. He had lost his place and was reading off cue cards.

I reminded myself I was here to try to find information to help Maya. These weren't classmates anymore. These were suspects.

Rose Nelson looked like a mourning queen, eyes dramatically downcast, beautiful and dusky. Her circle of hyper-attentive friends, some of them probably mourning Jefferson for secret reasons of their own, whispered worried thoughts in her ear.

Nearby, Rachael McHenry had been sobbing into the same tissue long enough that you could actually see her features through the wet paper. She was wearing a T-shirt with Jefferson's photo on it, with the date of his death — just three days ago — printed below.

Cheyenne had been holding my hand throughout the assembly, and I felt her fingers tighten when she turned to say something sharp to Sandra and Martine. I hoped she might be asking them to shut up, but then I heard her say that our teacher had promised there wouldn't be inverse functions on the quiz. I found their "business as usual" approach as irritating as Rachael McHenry's overdramatic sobs.

"You all need to stop," I said.

"Stop what?"

"Talking about math! It's disrespectful. Wait, never mind." The principal had left the stage, and apparently we were all supposed to be applauding. Who took his place but Brian, Jefferson's little brother.

"Tell me they're not having him talk to the whole school," Cheyenne said. "Awkward!"

Was it awkward? The gesture seemed moving, actually. He was fifteen, but looked younger. Really skinny, always wearing a crystal around his neck. Brown hair. Cute. Ill at ease. Today he was wearing a T-shirt with one of those creatures from fantasy movies, a lion with wings. He'd have been more than willing to tell anyone what it was called and what spells would be most effective against it, I was sure. On any day but today.

If Jefferson hadn't just died, the crowd would have started hooting and teasing. But as a group we were stumped about how to act, so everyone stayed quiet.

He looked miserable, twisting back and forth behind the microphone. Some guidance counselor had encouraged him to speak, I'm sure, as a way to bring the school together. But all that was happening was that we were drowning this grieving kid in silence. I started to clap, just to break the horrible moment. Only a few dozen other people took it up, but the show of support was enough to get Brian to start speaking.

"Thank you all for coming today," he said. "My family really appreciates everyone's help. We do." He took a big breath. "I think I'm supposed to say something about how death is both ugly and beautiful, how it's a big loss but at least it brings out the best in everyone. But Jefferson's death isn't like that. I'm supposed to say how wonderful he was, how he was an honor roll student, like it's better when kids like me, who aren't on the honor roll, die. So I'm not going to say anything wonderful about my brother."

He dragged out a pause, as if to emphasize some coming point of drama in his speech. You know how speakers will make you feel as bad as possible, only to swoop down and rescue the moment? But Brian just turned off the mike and left the gymnasium.

The principal was momentarily stunned and then took the mike and turned it back on. "Guidance is open. Come talk at any time. But for now, back to fifth period, everybody." A moan rose from the group. "Yes, there's twenty minutes left. Get going!"

After psychology, math was my favorite subject. Even so, there was no way in hell I was going to the second half of a calculus quiz — I couldn't work up any concern for math, not now. But I wasn't sure how to handle Cheyenne. If I said I didn't want to go to class, she'd insist on keeping me company, and I wanted nothing more than to be alone. So, as the girls headed down the hallway, I stopped at the main concourse. "I have to get my books and stuff."

They stood in a straight line, watching me nervously, like alien heads were about to erupt from my neck.

"For real. I'll be there in a minute. I just have to get my books! Why are you staring at me like that?"

"It's a quiz; you don't need a book," Cheyenne said.

"Don't worry about it. I'll. See. You. There," I said, and dashed into the crowd.

"Don't forget, cap and gown orders are due today!" Cheyenne called after me.

Of course I didn't head for the lockers, but instead went for the front doors of the school. I was pushing on the handle when I was stopped by a teacher — and the worst teacher to run into when you want to be alone. Mr. Duarte, hip clothes and an endless willingness to invade your personal space if it will get you to Talk About Your Feelings. He stood in front of the doors, a calm and sympathetic smile on his face. "Hey."

I'd fanned my keys between my fingers, like I was preparing to defend against a mugger. I let them fall into my pocket. "Hey," I said.

"I understand if you want to leave and spend this time alone or with your family. I'm not going to stop you. But listen: Maya's in my advisory group. She hasn't shown up for ages. Do you know why?"

I shook my head, mumbled something about her deciding to go for her GED.

"It's a trying time, and I want to keep an eye on all my kids. Well, I figured she might not be coming in for a while, since she was so close to Jefferson, and she should have a chance not to fail this year. I've put together a list of assignments from her teachers in case she wants to pass any of her classes. Do you think you could bring her textbooks home to her?"

"What do you know about her and Jefferson?" I asked.

"Why don't you come to my classroom, and we'll talk about it."

"No, thanks, Mr. Duarte."

He pressed a piece of paper into my hand. "Come by anytime. Meanwhile, stay around other people, okay? Don't go through this alone."

I stared down at the page. At the top was Maya's locker combo.

■ ■ ■

The locker was virtually empty; obviously, Mr. Duarte wasn't aware of precisely how rarely Maya had been coming into Xavier High this year. There was an actual dust bunny inside, along with a Manic Panic carton, three sporks, and some loose-leaf paper. And, wedged into the backside of the vent, a note folded into a football.

I unfolded it with trembling fingers.

Three lines only:

Monday, May 13th
5:00
30 Langdell, #40

That address again.

13.

I mapped the address on my phone as I drove. I would be heading to a downtown apartment complex just around the corner from Medusa's Den. I realized as I approached that it actually *was* Medusa's Den: the building had entrances on two streets. I bypassed the humming halogen storefront and walked up to a bent tin door, countless layers of paint over countless layers of graffiti. When I rapped my knuckles against it, the door eased open.

A guy was shooting up in the stairwell. He was older, sinewy, someone you'd expect to see in an apron smoking at the back door of a restaurant. I wasn't shocked as much as embarrassed that I'd intruded on a private moment. I said, "Oh, I'm so sorry," and backed out the door, then wondered at myself as I stood paralyzed on the stoop. I'd apologized for invading a junkie's personal space. How unequipped was I for the directions my life was heading?

"Hey, are you okay?" a woman's voice said. I turned and saw the most handsome woman I'd ever seen. Not handsome, like they call the women men overlook in Jane Austen novels, but a really cute guy wrapped into a woman. Tank top, triceps popping from the strain of carrying a canvas grocery bag, biceps tattooed with barbed wire. Long blonde hair yanked into a ponytail.

"Yeah, I'm fine," I mumbled.

She nodded and pushed open the door, then saw the junkie. There was a stream of curses and protests in Spanish as she hurled the guy out on the street. I had to press myself against the railing to avoid him.

The woman stood next to me on the stoop and watched the guy hobble away. "Never again," she yelled after him. "*Never again*, do you hear? You're shut off!" She turned to me. "I'm sorry, did he bump you on the way out?" Something about how she'd phrased her own question pleased her, and she smiled.

I shook my head. She looked at me quizzically. "I'm going to go out on a limb and say that someone probably sent you to me."

I shook my head again. My heart raced — she was about to ask what I was doing there, and I hadn't prepared a reason.

She looked into me, frank and disbelieving. "Okay, yeah," I lied. "Maya sent me."

She nodded sharply and started upstairs. "Come on up, then."

I stepped over the used needle in the stairwell and followed her up to the fourth floor. As she opened the door and ushered me in, I hesitated. It seemed like a really dumb thing to do, to enter some drug den as cheerfully as

Goldilocks. Especially when I hadn't really settled on my lie for being there. But if I didn't go in, I couldn't get to the bottom of this woman's connection to Maya.

The whole place looked familiar. Walls white and shiny. Furniture obscured by clothes and magazines. Crowded, just so extremely *inhabited*, almost pleasant in its chaos. The total opposite of my home. "Do you want a drink or something?" the woman asked.

"No, thanks," I said, placing myself on the edge of the couch as she unloaded groceries. We were in Keith's apartment; we'd entered on the opposite side.

"How's Keith?" I asked.

She paused, a jar of grape jelly in her hand. "I didn't know you'd met Keith."

I shrugged, just the way I thought Maya would have. "Well, you know."

"So, why did Maya send you?" she asked. "She got the note I had a runner stick in her locker, I guess?"

"You know, it's not the easiest time for her." I was worried — how much longer could I stay evasive? But I wasn't sure exactly what to say yet.

"What do you mean?" she asked, studiously putting away groceries.

I shrugged again. "You know."

"I'm sorry, *who* are you, exactly?" she asked.

Keith could be here, somewhere, or he'd come home and he'd recognize me. I couldn't lie. "Abby. Maya's sister."

I watched her debate whether to introduce herself. Then she did. "I'm Blake. So Maya sent her *sister* to deliver? Or did Jefferson send you directly?"

Oh my god. She thought Jefferson was still alive. I was in over my head — and I knew way too little about what Blake knew to play it off.

"Neither of them sent me, actually," I said. "Maya's in trouble."

"No kidding," Blake said. "Yeah, she is." She eyed the doorway. As in, what she'd be booting me out through in a split second. But then she barreled on. "She was in trouble the minute she got involved with that guy. He's the softest starter with the hardest endgame, you know what I mean? Lure 'em in and then squeeze."

I wasn't sure what she was talking about. That Jefferson got Maya infatuated and then dropped her? That made sense, but Blake's tone was too severe to be talking about romance.

"You realize you girls' little boyfriend owes me about fifteen thousand?"

I remembered the packet of drugs in Maya's bedroom. The implication was clearer, now. Jefferson was some heavy dealer and had gotten Maya involved. Blake was their supplier. And Jefferson hadn't been holding up his end of the deal.

"I get why Maya sent you," Blake said. "She's afraid to show her face — she thinks I won't be hard on you, since you haven't been involved. And I guess she's right, for now. Look, all I really want is my money. Whatever it takes. And I like Maya, I really do. But she needs to understand . . . you need to *make her* understand that just because this little problem's got Jefferson at its root doesn't mean that he's the only one in trouble. She's been getting her cut, which means that she can take a fall, too. Whether or not she devotes every minute of the rest of her life to avoiding me. You get that?"

"My sister doesn't owe you anything." It came out before I knew what I was saying.

"What the hell are you talking about? How can you be sure of that? Because I'm telling you, there seems to be a whole lot that you don't know. Why exactly are you here?"

"Jefferson Andrews is dead," I said.

"He sure is," Blake said, eyes shining.

"No. He's really dead. Somebody killed him."

Blake dropped the grocery bag to the floor and sat on the arm of the couch. I could see stray wisps of hair fallen out of her elastic, sun damage around her eyes. She smelled like leather and dandelions, some hip men's cologne. "You're not kidding, are you?"

I shook my head, soaking in Blake's reaction. Her shock looked genuine — but she was a drug dealer, after all; I had no idea how crafty someone like that might be. Treating Jefferson as if he were alive could have been some wily ploy to keep me off guard. Though for what purpose, I couldn't imagine. I took a deep breath. These waters were cold.

"You're not going to get any money from Jefferson, because he's gone. Here are the facts: You've got a chain of guilt connecting back to you. If the police don't figure it out on their own, they could always be given a nudge. I'm not threatening you," I continued, seeing Blake's darkening expression, "I just want you to know the facts. Obviously, I'm not accusing you of killing Jefferson. But I will do anything to protect my sister. And to do that I need to figure out who really killed him."

I could tell Blake got what I was saying. She was a drug dealer, but she also seemed fair, somehow. Honor among thieves. "He's definitely been killed, nothing ambiguous about it?" she asked.

"Yes."

"Then I hate to say it, but the top of your suspect list should be your sister. He was screwing with her mind, screwing *her*, getting her hooked on all sorts of stuff and then upping his rates, forcing her to deal to pay for what he'd already given her. He was a user, you know what I mean? In, like, a profound way. And of all the people he used, she was the one who was most wrapped up in it all."

"My sister didn't do it," I said. "That's out of the question."

"Look, you can be blind, if you want. But what you'd best do is keep her under the radar. It doesn't look good at all for her."

"You're afraid of what she'll say about you if she talks to the police."

"Why are you being such a little hawk?" Blake asked. "I think I'm being pretty helpful to you, given the circumstances."

"You just seem like someone with plenty to hide," I said.

"And you? You've got absolutely nothing to hide?"

I laughed. "Me? What are you trying to say?"

"Don't think that your sister wouldn't turn on you in a second," Blake said. "If it's in her best interest for you to be toast, you're toast."

It was beyond Maya's capabilities to hurt me like that. No, Blake was just trying to get me to give up. I had it in me to press for more, but I sensed I wasn't going to get any further with her today.

A key made a sound in the lock and Keith walked in from the tattoo parlor side. "What a day," he said. "I — Abby! Didn't expect to see you here again."

"Hi," I said. Keith reached out a hand, and I shook it. He gave Blake's shoulders a tender rub, and she reached back and placed her elegant fingertips over his. If he was surprised to find me there, he covered it up pretty quickly.

"How's Maya holding up?" he asked me.

Blake wheeled on him. "You knew about the Jefferson situation, too?"

"Yeah," he said. "Maya spent the night here after she left him. Got her Jefferson tattoo covered up earlier that evening."

He glanced in the wastepaper basket. "Oh, it's gone. She must have emptied the trash before she left. Uncharacteristically thoughtful of her."

"She had a Jefferson *tattoo*?" I asked, deflating.

"Not anymore, apparently," Blake said. "Were you going to tell me about all of this?" she asked Keith. "That Jefferson's *dead*?"

"It seemed like something to keep quiet," he said, kissing the top of Blake's head. "I know, I know," he said on top of her sputter, "let's talk it out later, okay?"

"Later is now," Blake said. "Abby was about to leave."

I stood up. "Apparently, I was about to leave."

"Look," Blake said, rubbing her forehead, "I'd say stop getting involved, but it's too late for that. So the best you can do now is to help us before we have to *force* you to help us. You know what I mean?"

Not exactly, but I certainly got the gist.

"Give the girl a break," Keith said warningly.

"I'm not saying anything," Blake said. "I merely want Abby to know that she should call us if she has any sort of contact with her sister."

"You really should get going, Abby," Keith said, looking nervously at Blake and opening the front door.

"You have one of our numbers?" Blake said.

I shook my head. Keith's number had been in Maya's phone.

Blake said her number. "You going to remember that?"

The way she'd said it, I'd have to work damn hard if I ever wanted to forget it.

But there was something more I had no intention of forgetting whatsoever:

Why hadn't Keith told Blake that Jefferson was dead?

TUESDAY, MAY 14

14.

Apparently, Mr. Duarte had called my parents to tell them I'd left. I told my dad that I'd skipped one class to be with my friends and talk things through. Dad, being Dad, insisted on escorting me to school on his way to work the next day. His official story was that he didn't want me to be by myself, but I knew he suspected I was going to skip again. I don't know how he does it, but he always seems to know everything about everything.

I'd have expected him to look all drawn and tired from worrying about Maya, but he seemed his usual self: whole, hardy, and fortressed. Maybe it was a front so I wouldn't get too worried. Or maybe even Maya's continued absence, like most everything else in his life, hadn't especially moved him. "Any word from your sister?" he asked as he drove. He'd asked me the exact same thing a few minutes earlier, but I did him the courtesy of checking my cell phone and saying no.

For once, I wasn't lying. There hadn't been any word from her. And I hadn't been able to get any more info out of Veronica. Luckily, the police didn't seem to be connecting Maya to the crime yet — not in a way obvious enough for any of us to realize, at least.

"Hey," my dad said as I got out of the car, "this is all going to be okay. You know that, right, honey?"

"I know, Dad," I said as I stepped onto the pavement of the bus circle. I let him watch me walk into the school . . . and then, as soon as he was gone, I came right back out.

I convinced myself that I'd take only an hour to myself and then start the day with second period. I'd just make a quick gas station run — the gas station being the only business within walking distance. It was brand-new and oversize, with a dozen widely spaced pumps and broad bays of halogen lights that made you feel like you were at some super-secret military base. Ernie the senile manager hadn't caught on to the stream of Missouri driver's licenses in the hands of high schoolers all born on the same day, so it was a favorite hanging-out ground for anyone cutting school and hoping for beer. I for one would usually get my gas, greet Ernie, and do my best to avoid the fattening chips and leering losers.

"Hi, Ernie, how's business?" I said this time as I paid for two of the largest bags of Twizzlers ever to exist. He adored me, maybe because I was the only high schooler who ever talked to him. He threw in a free lighter — I guess he figured all teens smoked — and I thanked him. "Yep, see ya later, Abby darlin'," he mumbled after me as I stepped outside.

The late bell rang in the distance. I watched a car pull up at the circle and a boy get out. Rather than entering the school, he headed toward me and Ernie and the space-age gas station. He walked right by me, went inside, and came back out, tapping a pack of gum against his wrist like it was cigarettes. It was Brian, Jefferson's little brother. I was struck all over again by his gawkiness. I saw his skull and not his head.

Brian wasn't the type to skip school, either. We were two good kids way out of our usual element. Instead of heading to class, I waved at him. I could use some tortured company.

"Hi," I said, in that heavy way of people in tragedies, tired beyond niceties but obligated to use them. "How are you holding up?"

Brian squinted back from beneath a weight. I'd never been friendly to him before. Few people had. "Not great," he said, fingers clenched around a backpack strap.

"I'm surprised to find you near school at all," I said.

He scuffed one shoe against the other.

"Aren't you supposed to be in counseling or something?" Did I really just say that? "Sorry, that was weird. Do you want to hang out with me for a while?"

I'm not sure he did want to, but it was beyond him to say no to me. His bag tumbled beside him as we sat on the pavement next to the used gas canisters. "I like your pins," I said, pointing to one at random, some pewter claw. I didn't like his pins. They just called for commenting.

"Thanks."

"Are your parents making you come to school?" I asked, with the called-for levels of frustration and disgust.

"Nope," he said. "I had to really fight to get to come. Actually, technically they said I couldn't. But they've shipped me off to my grandmother's for a couple days while they deal with everything, and I talked her into bringing me. I'd rather not be alone, know what I mean? Even though I'm totally ticked that you can't move in my parents' house without bumping into relatives asking how you're doing."

"You want to have company. But you don't want to be with anyone else, either," I said, nodding in the direction of the school.

"Yeah."

"I get that," I said, lying against a rusty canister and placing my hands over my face. I sure did get it — it was exactly how I was feeling those days. I could sense Brian shift position next to me — I felt him silently acknowledge that I was skipping school, too, and that it was unusual.

"Were you close to him?" Brian asked.

I started to nod, then thought about it and shook my head.

"Want to get out of here?"

This time I nodded enthusiastically.

15.

Brian and I didn't speak as we walked, and in our silence I tried to figure out why. He had to be way worse off than me. I had Jitters and Anxiety, my chattery companions since Friday night; he had Gaping Bruised Grief. I wondered if he was worried, too, if he could possibly feel anything thrumming beneath that thick numbness.

The Andrews family lived in a trailer park near the school. It wasn't like you might expect. The trailers were all pretty large, with multiple rooms and tidy lawns and curled green hoses in plastic holders and gnomes huddled in serious conversations. Of all the trailer parks in the city, it was by far the best. And the Andrewses owned not one trailer but two, one cube visible from the front and the other pitched on the reservoir slope in back. Both were surrounded by big and aggressive ferns.

We passed by the 1950s-style entrance with its metal cursive lettering and headed to Brian's trailer. The parents used the front one and the boys the back; we could go in Brian's without anyone else even knowing we were there.

Because their mobile home was on the slope, the boys' hallway had no natural light, just the occasional dull glow of motion-sensitive bulbs. It was a world apart from the scrubbed and illuminated upper trailer, which was full of red brick and pots and pans and pastel art purchased from carts in the mall. The boys' trailer was intimate and closed, like the space under a comforter. Once you pressed through the ferns, you were fully and thickly alone.

Brian creaked open the door to his room. The first thing I saw was a huge TV. On it, a pixelated man was frozen in mid-action. Red bar over his head, he was in the process of sawing away at a horde of monsters. Brian scrambled for the remote. "Sorry. This game'll let me pause but not save. So I just leave it running. Here we go." He clicked off the screen.

Slipping into a game world sounded like paradise. But it was weird, the idea that Brian was on day four of his brother being dead and he'd decided to decapitate goblins. I tried to remember the first stage of grief from AP psych. Commitment? No, that didn't sound right. Denial. That was it. Ah.

As Brian sat in his desk chair I kicked off my flip-flops and sat on his bed. He curled his knees up to his chest and peered at me, soul distant behind his glasses. I swung my hair around to one shoulder. Brian picked up on my flirtation and suddenly looked nervous. I got nervous, too. What the hell was wrong with me, flirting with Jefferson's brother, and now?

"I really need to —" I stopped speaking. A headache, which had been pulling on me all morning like tide on a swimmer, suddenly surged. I lay back into Brian's soft sheets, placed his pillow over my face. The pillowcase smelled like Jefferson, human oil plus a sweet chemical twinge of cheap gel. They must have used the same product, reached for the same plastic bottle along the same stretch of counter each morning. I felt the bed depress as Brian sat down next to me.

The need to connect to a person was filling me, radiating out like a physical force. My cheeks pulled tight and my scalp ached. I forced my hands to stay under my back. I hadn't ever been attracted to Brian. I wasn't attracted even then. But it felt exactly like it — I was so lonely. "I don't know what to do," I finally said, never removing the pillow so I wouldn't have to look into his eyes.

Brian didn't touch me, but I could feel the warmth of his hand hovering over my shoulders. "What don't you know what to do about?" he asked.

"You know Maya, right?"

"Yeah, sure. Why?"

"She's missing."

The mattress lifted, and I opened my eyes to see Brian up and pacing his room. "Are you thinking she had something to do with my brother . . . ?"

"No, of course not."

"I'm sorry your sister's missing," Brian said flatly.

"I don't expect you to worry about it," I said. We sat in puddled silence for a while. "But who do you think did it?"

"I'm not even thinking about that," he said. "Someone neither of us knows. A stranger. Jefferson screwed over plenty of people. It could have been any of them."

"What kinds of people?"

"I don't know, tons," Brian snapped. "I don't really want to talk about all my brother's bad history right now, okay?"

I searched the room for something I could use to change the subject. Immediately by the bed, there was a picture of Brian and his brother, outdone by a gleaming frame. They were little kids, dressed as soldiers. Jefferson had obviously pulled older brother privileges and kept the better gear for himself, dressed in fatigues and holding a play rifle, while Brian had a plaid shirt, tighty-whiteys, and a stick. It was sweet but also strange, for Brian to keep a picture of the two of them by his bed. Maybe he'd moved it to a more prominent position now that his brother was gone. The rest of the room: one shelf full of vampire books, another of graphic novels. Velvet curtains. Replicas of medieval weapons hanging over the doorway, two swords and a fancy steel club thing. I was surprised his parents let him keep them after the kids from my school cut each other up sword fighting for some role-playing game last year. It was a huge deal, and a group of parents petitioned to close the local hobby store. One of those TV vans with a tower coming out of its roof was parked outside our school for a week.

"So, the assembly . . ." I said.

Brian grunted.

I continued. "I mean, what —"

"I hated him. I totally and completely detested my brother." Brian groaned. There was some little war going on between two halves of him. "And you should have, too, based on what he put your sister through. So let's stop pretending that we're like the rest of the sorry dupes who think he's some shining star. It's a tragedy that he's dead. I'm in total shock, sure, but I'm not going to sit here and pretend that some small part of me isn't glad that he's gone, that I won't have him badmouthing me to the whole school, making it his mission to take down every friendship I made, humiliating me and framing me to my parents for all his shit."

"I had no idea he was doing all those things to you. That's terrible."

"No one noticed. I'd have told, but how was it going to help me at all to complain to any of you guys? Everyone already avoids me; I'm not fun, I get it. My parents knew a lot of what he was doing to me, but Jefferson knew how to work them, too. My dad would bitch him out and then within a few hours he'd be patting my brother's back, like he was actually proud of him for being such an ass to his weirdo little brother."

I guess I'd already suspected everything Brian was saying, but I hadn't ever really considered it too seriously, because I was also certain that Brian adored his brother. I'd seen the way he looked at him. He just wanted Jefferson to love and need him back, but since Brian was of no use to Jefferson, he never got anything from him. Cheyenne said once that Brian looked at Jefferson like Maya looked at me.

But that was ridiculous; I knew for a fact that Maya didn't idolize me. And it's not like I treated Maya like she was useless. Our situation was way more complicated than that.

In psychology class we learned that sociopaths are highly intelligent people who don't have genuine emotional reactions to situations but have become so skilled at faking their responses that they can appear normal even as they're steadily working on some secret agenda. If they seem upset or excited, the emotion is being *deployed* rather than *felt*. It makes them charming but also untrustworthy. I recognized Jefferson as soon as I heard about sociopaths. While Mr. Wachsberger read the description aloud from the textbook I watched Jefferson, looking for a reaction. He'd just finished punching his friend's leg, and the base of his throat was turning red from suppressed laughter. He wasn't even listening. *I see you,* I remember thinking. *I see into you, Jefferson Andrews.*

"He took people's weaknesses," Brian said, "and used them to his advantage. Cheyenne's vulnerability was schoolwork. Maya's was romance. Rose didn't want to suffer the humiliation of a breakup. He knew me best of all, of course, and so he trapped me the easiest. Got me into online gambling, and goaded me into higher and higher priced games until he had to bail me out with his drug money. So that I owed him. That's what he wanted; that was the end goal. For me to owe him."

"Why are you telling me this?" I asked.

His eyes darted over my face. "I trust you. And I'm miserable — talking should help, right?"

"I'm so sorry, Brian," I said. "This is just awful, isn't it?"

He let out a long guttering sigh.

"It's totally fine if you say no," I said slowly. "Really, really. But would it be creepy if I told you I wanted to see his room?" I asked.

Brian shook his head. I don't think "creepy" was ever an issue for him.

The room wasn't totally shut off, Brian explained, because the crime hadn't actually occurred there. There was just some police tape, and that was easy enough to duck.

Jefferson had a hot guy's room. Short gray carpet, orderly shelves lined with drab books and trophies. All his video games had sports leagues' insignias on the spines. His bed was made neatly enough that the pillows seemed to float an inch over the duvet. At one end of the room sat a glass-top desk with a laptop on it. "Shall we?" I asked, and strode to the center of the room before Brian could answer.

It didn't smell like Jefferson; it smelled like a room that had been closed off for too long. The air had died. But I twirled in it. A dead boy had lived here. It was a place of gravity and horror and splendor. I expected Brian to say something like "Abby, no," but he asked me if I wanted soda and then went off to get us some. By the time he came back, I'd turned on Jefferson's laptop. I had the pictures folder open. One image in particular was filling the screen.

Jefferson and Maya.

She was topless, sitting on his lap. He had on a tank top; it was nighttime on a beach somewhere. His near arm was straining to take the photo, biceps raised beneath his freckled skin. Maya's cheek was pressed against the edge of his backward Dolphins cap. They were both smiling hugely. I'd never seen her smile at anyone else like that.

"Would you take a look at that," Brian said, whistling.

I covered the screen with my hand. "They were totally on the down-low. You can't tell anyone, do you hear me?"

"When was that taken? Do you think Rose knows?"

"I don't know," I said. "Let's not worry about it," and dragged the file to the trash.

"You can't do that," Brian said. "This is officially police property or something."

"It's your house," I said. "I don't see any warrants or whatever. Brian, come on. You care about Maya, too. You know why I'm doing this." I dragged another file off the desktop.

"Oof," he said, sitting down on his brother's bed. "I don't feel too good."

I scanned the rest of the folder's contents and dragged the whole thing into the trash. But Brian's mentioning the police had gotten me to thinking. They had all sorts of labs to recover data, didn't they? It's not as though anything that was deleted was permanently gone. I knew that because we'd paid some guy a thousand bucks to recover my Vanderbilt essay in the fall. So the police would get the pictures no matter what. Unless I took the laptop. But Brian wouldn't let me, and even if he did I'd have incriminating evidence in my possession. Or . . . "Shit!"

"What? Oh no. God, god, oh god."

A good portion of a two-liter bottle of soda, all over the laptop. A Sprite lagoon with letter lily pads, an ice cube perched on the P. The screen clicked dark, with a sound like an old TV shutting off. When Brian lifted the laptop, fluid literally poured out. His arms sagged, the laptop spraying droplets on the carpet. "You did that intentionally."

"It was an accident," I protested, purposely lame-sounding, like I'd done something we should totally be laughing about.

"God," he said, placing the laptop back on the desk and ducking into the bathroom to grab toilet paper. "Who the hell cares, anyway? Do what you want. He's dead. Nothing's going to change that."

"If the police haven't gotten to the laptop yet," I said as he sopped up Sprite, "they'll assume it was always broken. Just play along. And in the meantime, we'll find out who really did it. Because Maya couldn't have. And you do really care, don't you?"

Brian shrugged. But I knew he cared about finding his brother's killer, no matter what shit Jefferson had put him through. If I were him I wouldn't be so sure that the police wouldn't think the computer had been sabotaged, though. But that was his issue. Brian wouldn't let them link it back to me; I'd make sure of that.

I did a visual scan of the rest of the room, looking for possible evidence. But Jefferson had already done the work for me, by keeping his secret life so under wraps from his parents. He'd covered his own tracks before I'd ever gotten there.

16.

As I left Brian's, I figured I'd head back to school, so I'd be waiting in front when my dad came to pick me up. As I walked I pulled my phone out of my purse; it had been chiming the whole time I was at Brian's. Each call was bound to be yet another stodgily concerned message from Cheyenne, and I wasn't ready to deal with her. But I hadn't expected three missed calls from my dad. Heart pounding, I listened to his messages. School had called and informed him I hadn't been in classes for a second day in a row.

I texted him to meet me in the school parking lot, and there he was, leaning against his car door, foot thumping. I was streaming excuses when I was still three parking spaces away. "I ran into Jefferson's brother on my way to first period, and he was so sad, his parents had made him go to school, and he couldn't deal, so we hung out and talked about stuff. Dad, I should have told you. I'm sorry."

A family meeting was declared as soon as we got home. Dad led me back into the dark, foreign den. Mom poured me a club soda. I thought the conference would be about how important it was that I go to school (I had a few defenses ready, a couple of them borrowed from the Maya playbook), but as soon as I'd taken my first sip Dad opened with this:

"The police are treating Jefferson Andrews's death as a murder investigation. Which makes it all the more important that we find your sister. Primarily to make sure she's okay, but also because if she's skipped town, it makes it look like she was in some way involved, and we need to plan how to handle it. "

I suspected my skipping school would not make the afternoon's agenda.

"A detective called here this morning. They want to talk to Maya. I asked them if it was because Jefferson was her tutor, and they seemed to think it was more than that. Was it?"

I shrugged. "I don't think so. I mean, she might have had a crush or something. But he had a girlfriend. It's not like they were going out."

"Well, according to the police, your sister was the last person to call Jefferson the night he died. It was a one-minute call, and he called her back. It was the last phone call he made. And she's missing. That doesn't look good. At all."

"So she called him," I protested. "That doesn't mean that she killed him. It just means she was connected to him. For all you know, she needed homework help."

Dad leveled me a glance. We both knew how unlikely that was. "Look," he said, "we just want your sister to be safe. But we also have to be concerned if the police are concerned. If she doesn't turn up soon, we'll all be under intense scrutiny. We'll have to hire a lawyer. This isn't my field."

"Did you let the detective know how little control of Maya

any of us have? Why do they have to investigate the rest of us?"

"The law's the law," my dad said. "Your mother and I have responsibilities under it. We all do."

"The good news," Mom finally chimed in, "is that we know for sure that Maya is alive. She called Jefferson's number the morning after the murder."

Oh. I had been the one who made that call. But of course I didn't say so. "Well, that looks good for her, right?" I said instead. "No one who killed Jefferson would call him a few hours later."

"The simple fact of the matter," Dad said, "is that we need to do everything we can to get Maya to come home and answer some questions. Even if we're not going to like the answers."

From the way he was talking, I knew she'd become guilty in my parents' eyes. It had happened as simply as that. Maybe they didn't think she was guilty of murder. But she was guilty of something.

"And I'm afraid that's going to come down to you, sweetie," Mom continued, nervously massaging her throat. "You have the best shot of all of us. We're calling everyone we can think of, but you know more about her circle and exactly who she's friends with. The police will go easy on her if she comes in for questioning on her own. But the more time goes by, the harder it's going to be. Until eventually they'll start assuming the worst."

"Unless one of us finds out who really did it first," I said.

"Of course," Mom said, glancing at my father. "But you mustn't do any investigating on your own, Abby. Promise us you won't. We don't want anything bad to happen to you."

That glance between them was pages long. They were terrified about Maya's well-being, but they'd also given up on her innocence. If she was sunk, they weren't going to allow their remaining daughter to taint herself.

"In the meantime," my father said, perching on the windowsill at the far side of the room, "the detectives need to speak to you."

I tried to hide my fear. "They want to talk to me? Is that normal?"

"Perfectly normal, darling," my mom said.

"The detective I talked to is named Tay Jamison," Dad said. "His partner is Raul Alcaraz."

"Don't look so worried, honey," Mom told me. "Answer their questions the best you can. That's all anyone asks."

"Just don't," my dad said after pausing, "give them any more information than they ask for. Respond to their questions, and that's it."

"When do I have to go see them?" I asked.

"They're coming here," Dad said. "In an hour."

"An hour?" I asked. I sounded alarmed, but I was actually relieved. I'd figured I'd end up talking to the police at some point, but I'd imagined having to go down to the station in a cruiser, handcuffed and led into one of those rooms with two-way mirrors.

"Don't worry," Mom said. "We'll be right here."

"Do you guys think Maya's okay?" I asked. It was funny — I said Maya but I sort of meant me.

Dad didn't say anything. Mom said, "I don't know." Her role in our family was always to put on a positive spin, and the best she was able to drum up was a simple "I don't know." She was despairing. I wanted to tell them, then, that Maya was okay, that Veronica had taken responsibility for her. But they couldn't know. And, oh god, the police couldn't know, either. Would I be able to pull this off?

"Do you know that we'd canceled Maya's tutoring with Jefferson just last week?" my father said. "Did your sister mention it?"

I shook my head.

"Your mother received a call from Mrs. Andrews, telling us that Maya had shown up at their place at three in the morning. That she'd knocked on Jefferson's window and then on Brian's, trying to get inside. Mr. Andrews had gone out to deal with her. He said she'd been hysterical, acting erratically, screaming over and over that she wanted to see Jefferson. So the next morning they called me and asked that I not allow her to see Jefferson again. And of course, that's the first thing that they told the police. I just wanted you to know in case the police bring it up."

"Why didn't you tell me before?" I asked softly.

"We didn't want to trouble you about all of your sister's doings. But now, because the police already know, you should be prepared."

"Well, I didn't know anything about it. That's what I'll tell them."

Dad nodded, more to himself than to me. "That's right."

"None of this looks good, honey," Mom said.

She had no idea.

17.

'd had an hour to compose myself, but I wasn't feeling any more collected by the time the detectives arrived. Their police car made a rumbling tread on the driveway, their parking brake an aborted squawk. I heard them chatting with my mom and dad, then the heavy noise of my dad climbing the stairs to fetch me. I opened the door before he could knock. "Where should I meet them?" I asked.

He hugged me. "Dining room okay by you?"

"Okay," I said.

"Don't be worried," my dad said again. He sounded like he was conferring with a legal client. I wondered if this was how he spoke to people he knew were guilty.

Alcaraz and Jamison were meaty guys in badly fitting polyester. Alcaraz had a face that was both pitted from some childhood acne and silky smooth, like an old glazed pot. He stood when I came in, shook my hand like a coworker's. Jamison had a bent spiral notebook out on the table, next to two mugs of coffee my mom had probably compelled them to accept. The mugs were green running into purple with broken gray veins, all slathered in a clumpy glaze. Maya and I had made them at camp a few years before. Mom, no doubt, had used them to remind the police officers that the suspect they were after was someone's daughter. Good one, Ma.

"Let's sit down," Alcaraz said. He pointed to the chair opposite him. I paused and then lowered myself in. He'd placed me where Maya usually sat, though he couldn't have known that.

My parents were hovering at the entrance to the dining room. I could sense their fear that they'd be sent away, that the detectives would ask to question me alone. My dad was leaning against the doorway, a comradely look on his face, as if we were all at a company picnic.

"We don't have to take this one alone, do we, Raul?" Jamison asked his partner.

Raul shook his head. My mom started to sit.

"I'd rather we did," I said.

Jamison looked to my dad. "No objection, Mr. Goodwin?"

Dad gave me a long, questioning look, then shook his head and led Mom out of the room. Once they'd shuffled away, stunned, Jamison and Alcaraz sized each other up and pencils came out.

"Any reason you don't want your parents here for this, Abby?" Jamison asked.

"I want to be as open as I can," I said. "I don't want to have to think about them at the same time as I'm trying to remember things. Besides, there's stuff about Maya I'm sure they wouldn't want to hear."

They looked at each other hungrily. "Let's get started, then!" Jamison said. "I'm sorry about Jefferson. Your life must have turned absolutely upside down in the last week, huh?"

"It's been crazy," I said lamely.

"It's amazing," Jamison said. "We haven't found anyone who didn't feel very deeply about him. He touched so many lives. Had such an impact for such a tragically short life."

I nodded.

"When did you first get to really know him? I mean, we assume you first met him in school."

"First day of kindergarten, yeah."

"But when did he start coming into your home?"

"You're talking about his tutoring Maya, right? She was bombing classes, cutting school. When did that reach its peak? Gosh. About a year ago. My parents asked me if I knew anyone who could come by and help. Jefferson's really smart, and I'd heard his family didn't have much money, so he was the first person I suggested. My parents arranged it all with his parents, and he started coming over a few times a week. They did their work right here at this table. He sat where you are, Detective Alcaraz. Just there."

He looked at his seat and fixed me an unknowable smile. "How did your sister feel about him?"

"What do you mean?"

"Whatever you take me to mean."

The key here, I knew, was to get close enough to the truth for it to be believable, but leave out the parts that would implicate her further. I had to tread very, very carefully.

"At first," I said, "she was just pissed that she was getting tutored. She thought she didn't need it. She was failing practically every class, but there you go, that's how my sister thinks. It turns out, though, that Jefferson was a perfect choice. She liked him enough that even if she'd have skipped school the whole day, she'd show up to make her tutoring session."

"Did she have a romantic connection to Jefferson Andrews?" Jamison asked.

Yes? No? I opted for uncertainty. "I don't know."

"Really?" Alcaraz said.

That question let me know that a romantic connection was the reveal they were grasping for.

"Really," I said, looking him straight in the eye.

"Okay, let's cut through the bull," he said. "Your sister is on the run. You can protest as much as you like, but it won't change the fact that as far as we're concerned, the fact that she is a fugitive is undeniable. And while she's on the run, it's virtually impossible for us to look at her as anything but a suspect. Now, no one's going out of their way to say she killed Jefferson. But maybe she witnessed something she wished she hadn't and can't bring herself to face us. We honestly don't know. But I have to tell you, the clock is running down. Within seventy-two hours we will present formal charges against her. And then the game changes entirely. Her picture gets distributed to all the police in the state, and most likely the FBI gets involved. If your sister turns herself in, or is turned in, before those seventy-two hours are up, then we can work with her on the local level. If we find out that she was coerced, or she simply screwed up and is embarrassed to come forward, we'll do our best to minimize the charges. Three days from now, that offer will be in the past. But we have no way of letting Maya know all of this if we can't get in touch with her. You see our predicament."

"We've talked to your father," Jamison said, looking at me sympathetically. The rough skin around his mouth fell into heavy lines. "We know his struggles with Maya, and how she would probably never approach him on her own —"

"But a sibling is different from a parent. We find it hard to believe that you don't have a very good idea of exactly where she's hiding," Alcaraz said. "Don't try to deny it," he said, putting up a hand. "Because you do *not* want to start lying to us. We're not expecting you to give up your sister. All that we want," Alcaraz continued, "is for you to pass a message to her. Let her know that if she turns herself in immediately, we'll all do our best to make this end as easily as possible. If she waits until even Friday, she's dealing with a national investigation of first-degree murder. And at that point there will be nothing we can do."

I nodded. "If I manage to get in touch with her, I'll do what I can."

Alcaraz took a card out of his back pocket and slid it across the dining table. "Keep this in a safe place, okay? And don't hesitate to call me."

I slid the card into my pocket. "Are we done?"

They glanced at each other. "For today."

"Then have a great day." I spun out of the room.

It made me mad, that they had a plan for me that I couldn't know about except for the scraps I could infer from their questions. The police had access to information that I didn't, of course, but it made me furious that they didn't just tell me everything they knew. Much like it probably made them angry that I clearly hadn't told them everything *I* knew.

They didn't leave right away, of course. My mom chitchatted with them in the kitchen, refilling their mugs and asking about Alcaraz's wife, Jamison's boyfriend, their webs of children and nieces and nephews. It seemed like aimless chatter, but Mom always had a plan. She kept the conversation focused on what they all shared: family, loyalty, morality. Then my dad joined in. Cheerful, jokey legal talk. Alcaraz brought it back to the murder by asking whether my dad minded if they had the phone company subpoenaed for the records on Maya's line. I guess my dad said yes, I couldn't hear. All the while I was sitting in the dining room, sifting through everything I'd said, searching for anything I might have given away. But in the end I was satisfied; I'd done the best I could. The police left, and Mom joined me in there, hugged me where I sat. Her necklace rattled against my head; I smelled her perfume and felt the roughness of her thick bra beneath her shirt. I was really glad for her company.

She left, and as I continued to sit in the dining room, I could hear heavy banging in the basement below. From Maya's room.

Once the policemen were gone, I opened the door to the basement. "Dad?"

Only more banging in response.

I ran down the stairs. He was hurling open drawers, scattering books and papers and clothes.

"Dad?" I called out, clutching the banister. He still didn't seem to hear me.

He had finished searching the rest of the room and had worked his way to the bed, lifting the frame so it rested on his back. He didn't even seem to notice its weight; he looked like a bear raiding some unlucky animal's nest. "What are you doing in here?" I asked.

"Get out!" he bellowed, not even turning around. Shredded cardboard boxes were piling up at the side of the bed. The *A* volume of the encyclopedia was already tossed to one side.

"You're scaring me!" Appealing to compassion wasn't going to get me anywhere, given the state my dad was in, and I should have known it. There would be no stopping him.

"No!" my dad roared. He had found the mushy brown brick under the bed. He turned to me, the drugs held in his hand like some dead creature. "Did you know about this? Was this why you wanted to talk to Alcaraz and Jamison alone?"

I was already halfway up the stairs. "No!" I yelled. "I wanted to talk to them alone because of this kind of stuff! Because of your temper, Dad!"

"Go and wait with your mother. I'll be there in a minute."

I lingered.

"Now!"

I fled, eyes stinging. The laundry room was right next to the basement entrance, and I stood there for a moment. Cody, penned in by the dog door, pressed herself against me. She knew something was wrong, and whimpered and stared at me concernedly. There was no way I was sticking around to deal with my dad's anger. I got why he was mad, what colossal pressure he was under with Maya missing, the tension that must be boiling in him from the conflict of wanting to do the right thing and yet see that his daughter was safe. His rage was coming from a fatherly place, but that didn't mean I wanted to deal with it. As soon as she realized what was going on, Mom would start working to calm him down, but until she'd succeeded he would be yelling about how everything was my fault: *You should have known your sister better. We've done all we could as parents; why haven't you done better for her?* What he'd really be mad about, of course, would be not having been a good enough father to catch Maya earlier, for allowing her rebellion to get to the point where she was able to stay away for days at a time. But he wouldn't calm down until tomorrow at the earliest. In the meantime, living in my house would be hell. And I couldn't handle staying around him, not given the fragile trick I was trying to pull off.

I yanked open the dog gate, grabbed my keys, and

slammed out the door before my parents could ask where I was going. Delighted by this chaotic turn of events, Cody jumped into the passenger seat. I sped to the subdivision exit. As soon as the light went green I peeled out, sped down the service lane, and was gone.

As I did, though, I passed a string of cars — and there, at the head, was a cruiser with Alcaraz and Jamison in front. They turned their heads as I whizzed past. Spotted speeding away by the cops: fantastic.

18.

I pulled into the mall and left again through a side entrance, turning toward Cheyenne's house. I spent the whole drive staring into the rearview mirror. The cops didn't follow me, thank god, but I'd have to be more careful. Now I wished I hadn't been so curt at the end of their interview. Strong work, Abby.

I phoned from my car and asked Cheyenne to meet me out front. There was a trail near her house that we always walked along whenever one of us had something to discuss. I met her at the start, Cody straining on her leash.

"Where the hell have you been?" she asked right away.

"Great. Thanks. Helpful. Leave off the annoyingness for just a minute, okay?"

"Where have you been, sweet pea?" Mock sweetness. Rock sugar.

"Much better. Just had a major blowout with my dad."

We started walking. I let Cody off the leash and she immediately streaked away. "What now?"

"The police came by to interrogate me —"

Cheyenne turned pale. "What?"

"It wasn't that huge of a deal."

"What did you tell them?"

"Just that I didn't know any more than my parents did. Then, afterward, my dad got suspicious and raided Maya's room and found the hard stuff."

"What hard stuff? You mean hard drugs? Thanks for not mentioning that before. You know, when you weren't calling me back."

I waited the five seconds it took for her outrage to fade and then told her about my fight with my dad and more about the interrogation. I finished by apologizing that my mind felt all scrambled these days in the hopes that she'd take pity on me and stop picking a fight.

"And where exactly *is* Ms. Maya now?" Cheyenne asked.

I stopped. We'd been walking along abandoned railroad tracks, and I'd begun to sense that the scrub brush at the edge wasn't as empty as it looked. "Do you feel like we're being watched?"

I expected Cheyenne to snort and begin teasing me, but she nodded. "Yeah. I have for a little while, actually."

I looked back along the hazy tracks to where we'd come from. "Oh my god."

Right by my car was a figure, solitary and hooded. Almost in the tree line. Not moving. Just staring through the fog.

"Who the hell is that?" Cheyenne asked. "Hello?" she yelled.

The figure just stood there staring, then quietly moved off into the woods.

"Holy shit," I said.

"Don't be a drama queen. It's just some loser in a hoodie."

"There's no way we're going back that way."

"Then we won't. We'll loop around the far side."

We wound up crossing through a fast-food parking lot. Cody emerged from the trees, and I tied her to a bike rack. We went in, got some dinner and coffee, and sat in a booth. I couldn't help looking over my shoulder, but no one in a hoodie followed us inside.

"Do you think school's getting back to normal?" I asked, in an attempt to get *me* to feeling back to normal.

"No. Not at all. And other times, totally. Like at lunch. You'd think there'd never been a Jeff Andrews, the way everyone's back to yelling and flirting and throwing food. But during morning announcements, we hear about nothing else and everyone looks like they've just been gassed."

"And what's everybody saying happened?"

"We always tell each other the truth, right? Cheyenne and Abby against the world?"

I nodded.

"They're saying that Maya killed him. Like, *everyone*."

"Great. Just great. Where do you think that rumor's starting from?"

"The queen bee, who else? I didn't think Rose knew about Jeff and Maya, but from the way she's been acting, I guess she did. Not that she'd ever admit that Jeff was cheating on her. No, in her version, Maya's a stalker, and Jeff's the noble gentleman who kept turning her down."

"And people *believe* that?"

Cheyenne shrugged. "It makes it a juicy story if Maya killed him out of unrequited love, and people love a good story. But does anyone really believe that Jeff wasn't getting his hands dirty, so to speak? No way. There's a long train of girls who would testify that he was hardly faithful to Rose."

"I wonder how Rose could put up with all of that," I said. "Unless, of course, she suddenly couldn't."

"You think *Rose* might have done it?"

"Well, if she's got enough presence of mind to take time out from her grief to label my sister a murderer . . . I don't know. Let's face it — there are plenty of girls who've had moments where they wanted Jefferson dead. It's just a matter of having an opportunity. I mean, he's a big guy. But if someone stumbled on him when he was already hurt . . . What if he said the wrong thing? And all anyone would have to do would be to clobber him once and it would be over."

"You think he was caught with his pants down?"

"Well, it all depends on whether Caitlin — or whoever the other girl was — stood him up, right? Like, when she showed up after Maya left."

"Interesting," Cheyenne said. "Very interesting."

I was studying her reaction. I wanted to ask her why she had posted on Jefferson's page. Why she called him Jeff. Whether she'd ever had a crush on him herself. But there seemed to be no way to get to there from here. I sensed there was something she was holding back, but I couldn't figure out how to uncover it.

She took a sip of her coffee. The Styrofoam cup puckered under her strong fingers. "It hurts my feelings that you don't keep me closer during all of this. I want you to share where you're going, what you're finding out. You can't do all of this alone."

"I know, I know," I said. "But I just can't talk about all this crap anymore. Tell me about you. Everything about you."

"I don't want you to think it's your fault, but I lost my job at the mall."

"Oh god, that totally *is* my fault. I'm so sorry."

"Honestly, don't worry about it. Because there's some other great news. But jeez, it feels creepy even to talk about it, with everything that's happening to your family."

"Please. Distract me."

"I got into University of Miami."

"Cheyenne! That's huge!" I couldn't get überexcited, though. She'd long had her heart set on Miami, but it was a private school and cost way more than her parents could afford. Like, many thousands more. She'd been deferred early decision, so we'd started to think it wasn't going to be an issue, and she'd just go to a state school.

"You don't need to look so worried. I'll get the Florida's Scholars."

Florida's Scholars was a bunch of money given to the

valedictorian of every public school, if she stayed in state for college.

"You can't tell anyone," she said. "I don't want people looking at me funny."

I nodded. But still — Cheyenne was going to her dream school precisely because Jefferson was no longer eligible for valedictorian. I didn't know whether to be excited or outraged. My body hedged the difference and went for queasy instead.

"God," Cheyenne said, staring long and hard at the dollar menu. "I thought you'd be happy for me."

"Yes, no, absolutely. It's incredible news. But you shouldn't tell anyone. At least not until the current mess is sorted out."

"Are you saying I shouldn't have told you? My best friend?"

"Of course you should have told me. But you know how this looks."

"Wait!" she barked, spilling her coffee all over the table. Her mouth shut, and we stared at the steaming puddle. Neither of us moved to clean it up. I listened to drops of coffee plunking onto the plastic booth seat as I waited for Cheyenne to continue. "I know you want to keep your sister safe, Abby. But you're going too far when you turn on the one person who's always been on your side. First you cut me out, then you slam into me and start accusing me of . . . I don't even know what."

"I wasn't accusing you of anything. What are you getting so defensive for?"

"There you go, accusing me all over again. You can't even say you're not accusing me without accusing me even more. It's not like I went and proposed myself for Florida's Scholars. Mr. Roth called them once Jeff was dead, told them we had a new first in class. I didn't tell him to."

A tableful of old ladies was staring at us. Even the drive-through girl had frozen while passing a drink through the window. I couldn't breathe too well, suddenly. "Let's go, okay?"

"It's easy for you," Cheyenne said. "You say you're not the most popular girl, but you still make friends left and right. But no one really bothers getting to know me. I've only got you. So I'm sorry if I can't let it roll off my back when you turn on me. I'm not like you. I can't go hang out with someone else for a week. There *isn't* anyone else."

"I wasn't turning on you. Can't you understand that this is a totally impossible time for me right now? Why are you being so self-centered?"

"*Me* self-centered? You don't want to get into a self-centered contest, because you'll lose. Majorly."

I simply wasn't ready to fight with Cheyenne today. My resources were stretched so thin. So I did what I thought would get her to stop. "Please," I whispered. "I'm sorry. Let's let it go for now."

"Okay," Cheyenne said. "I'm sorry." But she wasn't. And I wasn't. Because if either of us had actually been sorry, we'd have found something else to say to each other. But we didn't; we just sulked and stared at the dark stain spreading on the tabletop.

Cheyenne left before I did. When I finally mopped up the spill and dragged myself outside, the hooded figure was back, staring at me from across the parking lot.

19.

He didn't seem as creepy this time. Maybe the light from the streetlamps was better; maybe it was just that he was closer. I still couldn't see his face — he was standing within the razor shadow of an abandoned store — but I had an instant suspicion of who he actually was. His hoodie had a giant many-sided die on it, for one thing. The kind that, back before she got into drugs, Maya might have rolled to see whether she'd hit a dragon with a +1 longsword.

I watched him from the exit door, buffeted by people entering and leaving. Our looks started the conversation.

Me: *Tell me you're not following me.*

Him: *Sure am. Sorry.*

Brian waited for me to cross the lot. "I saw Cheyenne leave just now," he said, throwing back his hood.

"Let's go," I said, scanning around to check whether we'd been seen. "My car's at her place. Can you give me a ride over to your neighborhood?"

"I had to return the car before my parents saw it missing. And I shouldn't be driving, anyway. I've only got my learner's permit." He said it like we were close, like we had some reason to know each other's birthdays and habits.

"Well, then, let's get walking," I said sharply.

"You okay?" he asked after I'd untied Cody and we were passing back into the park. The sun had fully gone down by now, so we stuck to the lighted path that arrowed between the dark trees.

"Life's been totally wonderful lately. How 'bout you, champ?"

He smiled. "You're cranky."

"And you're annoying. But we knew that."

I bit my lip. Last thing I wanted was another fight. But Brian seemed to brighten. I'd shown him the same callousness Jefferson had always shown him, no doubt. Maybe I'd made him feel nostalgic.

"What've you been up to lately?" I asked him.

"Mmm . . . not much."

"Did the, um, laptop issue cause you any trouble?"

"Nah. No one's noticed yet. The police will probably take the computer into evidence someday, but until then, no one will know."

"Have you even been home?"

"Oh yeah, I've been staying there instead of my grandma's. She does her best to take care of me, but she's too old for it and usually forgets I'm even supposed to be there. And my parents mean well, but they're a bit distracted. Well, a lot distracted. I'm taking care of myself these days. Lots of pizza delivery."

"And have the police been by much?"

"I guess so. Not while I was around. They talked to me the day after Jefferson's body was found, but I guess they've been busy following leads since then."

I told him about Alcaraz and Jamison coming by to talk to me. "If I don't track down Maya soon, there'll be trouble. Three days until the Feds get involved." *Feds.* What a heavy word.

"You don't have any idea how to locate her?"

I shook my head. "It's killing me."

"Online?"

"She hates the internet. And I'm sure the police and my parents are flooding her with messages. But yeah, I'll try that first."

"If you find her, maybe I could just hide out with her wherever she is. I can barely even fit in my parents' trailer. It's clogged with flowers and wreaths and casseroles and stuffed bears." He chuckled ghoulishly. "It's become the Jefferson memorial."

Brian walked with me to Cheyenne's house, where we piled Cody into my car and drove over to his place. I sent the dog out back, and he spent the evening showing me how to make some Chinese warrior chick throw fireballs. My phone kept buzzing and wheezing, ignored in my bag. I glanced at it occasionally, while Brian was fighting. Dad three times, Mom twice, Alcaraz once, Cheyenne once. I didn't check any of the messages, though each one pushed me further and further into my funk. The more that came in, the harder it was to start listening to any of them. Brian and I withdrew into our own world for a few hours. I was really grateful for his company, for the privacy of his trailer hidden within the leaves, for the worlds we escaped to in his video games.

"How did you get your parents to pay for this huge TV?" I asked as he electrocuted some hairy Russian dude.

"Oh," he said. He paused, and I wasn't sure if it was because he was vying for time or trying to execute some special move. "They didn't. Jefferson did."

"That was awesome of him."

"Um, kinda." The announcer declared the next fight was going to be incredible.

"Kinda?"

"Yeah. Kinda."

"Why just kinda awesome?"

"There was no such thing as a free gift with Jefferson, you know? Just ask Maya. She knows all about that."

"Um, I can't ask Maya, remember? So I guess you're going to have to fill me in."

"I said I wanted my own TV, and my parents said absolutely not. But there was a delivery at the door a couple of days later. You can guess from who, and how he got the money."

"Jefferson. From dealing."

"Atta girl. And then I owed him. That's what he loves, to make you indebted. After that he'd start having me keep his books. He'd give me a package to deliver, some sketchball to go talk to because he didn't have time or just didn't want to take the risk. And he didn't threaten to take the TV away, but he knew I owed him. So yes, Jefferson *gave me a TV*. It was *awesome* of him." A fat sumo guy was whaling on Brian, his hands flying everywhere. "So," he continued, changing the course of the conversation as the death countdown started ticking, "Cheyenne seemed pretty upset when she left."

"Uh-huh," I said, picking up the controller as the game went back to the main menu. "How do I get back to the Chinese girl again? I like her laugh. She's such a bitch."

"I figured Cheyenne'd be on cloud nine these days," he said. He took the controller and chose her for me.

"You heard about the Miami thing?"

"No. What do you mean?"

"Oh, what do *you* mean?"

"That AP scandal."

"What? I have no idea what you're talking about," I said.

"Oh, I forgot you weren't in Euro. You know how Jefferson and Cheyenne used to help each other on assignments last year? He'd give her quiz answers from first period, if she'd tell him what was on the bio test, that sort of thing? Well, she got nailed for plagiarizing an entire paragraph of a practice AP essay. She got sent to the principal, but since it was her first time she got off easy. But that paragraph hadn't been from the web — it'd been from Jefferson. She never told you this?"

No, she hadn't. "And *he'd* gotten it off the web?" I said.

Why hadn't Cheyenne ever said anything? A more searing sadness was replacing my earlier funk.

"Yeah, and then tipped off the teacher. It was a total setup."

"For what?"

"Cheyenne's from the same neighborhood as us. He knew she had no money. Getting valedictorian and Florida's Scholars meant so much to her. If she was banned from it, it would ruin her."

"And he wanted to be valedictorian instead."

"Sort of. Honestly, he probably couldn't have cared less about the actual title. It was more that he wanted her to be indebted to him. He knew she was insecure about her writing, and he'd been feeding her essays all year, in return for her letting him copy her calculus. He'd slipped her five more plagiarized essays, all from that same site. I know because he'd gotten me to find them. All he had to do was breathe a word, and Cheyenne would have been expelled. He had her at the drop of a hat."

"Why did he do it?"

"Because he could get her to do anything for him. Because it was fun. Really, there didn't need to be a 'why.' Putting her in danger *was* the point."

"I died," I said, pointing at the screen. I'd forgotten how to do that fireball thing.

It was so ironic. Cheyenne had accused me of withholding from her, but then Jefferson had been dangling this heavy stuff over her and she hadn't said a word. What a total hypocrite. I wanted to go confront Cheyenne right away, but then I thought better of it: Shouldn't I wait and think first about the position this new information put me in? Would the police believe that Cheyenne had killed Jefferson? Did I *want* the police to believe that Cheyenne had done it? Then Maya would be scot-free, after all. I prayed I wouldn't have to make a choice between my sister and my best friend. Alcaraz's card was still stiff in my pocket.

Brian's door opened, and in walked his dad, a tall, gruff, khaki guy with a bald head and a tendency to wear marathon T-shirts. "Oh, I'm sorry," he said when he saw me sitting on the bed. "I didn't realize." He closed the door, and then immediately opened it again. "Abby Goodwin? What are *you* doing here this late?"

"Hi, Mr. Andrews," I said, with a little wave.

His eyes were surrounded with this crazy purple color, grief and insomnia and sudden age. "Brian," he said, "what did we say about this? Unbelievable. I'll talk to you later. In the meantime, Abby, you have to leave. Right now. No guests."

"Okay," I said, standing. Mr. Andrews was well known for his temper — he'd once famously reamed out Brian in the middle of the parking lot, in front of the whole school. It'd ended with a loud slap that no one had told guidance about, though we'd talked about whether we should. I wasn't about to test his limits today.

"Dad!" Brian said. "Chill out. Abby had nothing to do with it."

"I don't care what you think you know. I'm sorry, I have to ask you to leave, Abby."

"What, I'm not allowed to hang out with anyone at all now?" Brian said. "Do you care at all what *I* might be going through?"

"Of course I do. But I'm not going to discuss this right now, do you understand?"

I watched Mr. Andrews's jaw muscles do this crazy wavy thing. Brian caught his father's dangerous vibe, too. "I'm sorry, Dad," he said meekly. "Can I at least walk her out?"

Mr. Andrews's hand clenched on the doorknob. Finally, he nodded.

"Let's go," Brian said. He powered down the game system and we ducked under his dad's arm to get out. I could feel Mr. Andrews's eyes on my back as we hurried down the hallway.

"He seems really worked up," I whispered. "But I can't imagine what it's like to lose a son."

"I don't think he can, either," Brian said. Which was a weird thing to say. But then again, weird was Brian's normal. "That's only half of what's on his mind. We're totally out of money."

I stuttered, unsure of how to phrase what I wanted to ask. "You mean for the funeral? Is someone dying expensive?" Surely that hadn't been the best way to put it.

"I guess," Brian said. "But even given that, it seems serious. Money's all my parents ever seem to talk about. Even though their son just *died*."

We were at my car. I wanted to ask Brian more, but I looked back and could see the blinds at the window rustle, like someone was watching. It wouldn't do any good to get Brian any more in trouble than he already was.

I also couldn't help but wonder if the reason I was being kicked out was because I was Maya's sister, and that Mr. Andrews had heard the rumors.

"Has Rose been by a lot?" I asked.

Brian groaned. "God. Rose. Before, she'd never bother to come here, because her house is, you know, so much more *comfortable*. But the minute he's dead? Suddenly, his house is the best place in the world for her. My mom actually had to go see her mom and explain that our family needed time to grieve alone. I don't think Rose took that very well, but at least she isn't coming by anymore. One of the reasons I keep dreading school is that if she sees me, I know I'm never going to get her to stop talking."

"I can understand that," I said.

"Yeah," Brian said. "I know you can."

"Call me later?" I asked.

"Yeah," he said.

"I wish your parents weren't being so awful," I said.

"Just come by," he said. "Secretly. You know my entrance. I keep a key inside that urn at the back door. I'm going to youth symphony rehearsal tomorrow night, but I'll be back by eight. My parents are in bed by ten. You could come over anytime after that. We could play games. Or maybe go have some coffee together or something."

"I'd like that, Brian. I'd really like that," I told him, then added, "Keep your eyes and ears open. If you hear anything about Jefferson and Maya, let me know."

He nodded. As he walked away, I called Cody and stroked her head and held open the passenger door, my thoughts churning.

I now had a man — well, a boy — on the inside.

WEDNESDAY, MAY 15

To: Maya Goodwin

From: Abby Goodwin

Hey. Just wanted to check in. Veronica won't tell me where you are, do you know that? Anyway, she's probably got you staying with one of her friends or something, and your phone is shut down, but I bet you're going online, anyway. Always do it on some public wireless network, though, okay? Because the police can track stuff like that. Wait, you just came online.

CHAT INITIATED

AbbyNotShabby (3:53pm): Hey Maya, it's me.

MayaPants10 (3:57pm): Sry, just noticed this. Was reading ur message. Who r u?

AbbyNotShabby (3:57pm): Thank god ur there. Its Abby. Don't you recognize the screen name?

MayaPants10 (3:58pm): prove it.

AbbyNotShabby (3:58pm): For real? You were born May first. You went to Xavier High until you dropped out.

MayaPants10 (4:01pm): not good enough.

AbbyNotShabby (4:01pm): You have four matching pink and black striped mini-tees.

MayaPants10 (4:03pm): u could have seen that.

AbbyNotShabby (4:03pm): M! It's me. You call me "Shabby" when you're mad at me. I made fun of you majorly for getting all four of those shirts. Mom would only pay for two, and you borrowed forty bucks to get the other ones. You still haven't paid me back, btw.

MayaPants10 (4:04pm): hey.

AbbyNotShabby (4:05pm): HOW ARE YOU??!!!

MayaPants10 (4:05pm): fine.

AbbyNotShabby (4:05pm): WHERE ARE YOU??!!!!

MayaPants10 (4:07pm): cant tell u.

AbbyNotShabby (4:07pm): For real? Are you someplace secure?

MayaPants10 (4:07pm): yes. Stop worrying.

AbbyNotShabby (4:10pm): Anyway. I know V canceled your cell phone, but you can call me if you want. From a pay phone. You have to tell me where you are. It's not safe if no one knows at all. What if something happened to you? I'd never forgive myself.

MayaPants10 (4:12pm): alright, shabby. calm that stuff down.

AbbyNotShabby (4:12pm): Do you think all of this is funny?

MayaPants10 (4:12pm): no deffinately not.

AbbyNotShabby (4:13pm): The police want me to give you up.

MayaPants10 (4:13pm): r u going 2?

AbbyNotShabby (4:13pm): Of course not. I wouldn't ever.

20.

MayaPants10 (4:13pm): thx.

AbbyNotShabby (4:14pm): but they say they'll go easier on you if you turn yourself in.

MayaPants10 (4:14pm): uh, yah! that's how they GET people to turn themselves in.

AbbyNotShabby (4:14pm): exactly. You have to stay away. For good, maybe. You think you can handle it?

MayaPants10 (4:14pm): ive run away b4.

AbbyNotShabby (4:14pm): yeah, but then you could always come back. You always DID come back. And you didn't have the police coming after you.

AbbyNotShabby (4:17pm): If you ran away Jefferson's murder would just be what, left permanently unsolved?

AbbyNotShabby (4:18pm): Maya. you still there?

AbbyNotShabby (4:18pm): maya?

AbbyNotShabby (4:22pm): . . . ?

AbbyNotShabby (4:29pm): Call me. Let me help you. And stay away, okay?

I conducted the chat in the parking lot of a Target, sitting in my passenger seat and leeching wi-fi. I closed the laptop and fiddled with the car radio for a while, I guess searching for a song so mind-blowingly awesome that it would carry me away from my worries. But a song that powerful doesn't exist.

I'd had no idea that the police would set their focus on Maya so early, and so thoroughly, and that my parents' sympathies would so quickly peel away from her. She was heading into a storm, and I was the only one who could do anything about it.

It was the end of the chat that got to me. Why'd she stop typing? I hadn't gotten a firm promise from her: Was she planning on coming back? What would I do if she didn't stay on the run, if she insisted on putting herself in danger?

In order to prove her innocent, I'd have to prove someone else guilty.

I sat in my locked car and listened to the slurry of voice mails on my phone. I deleted three angry rants from my dad, then listened to my mom pleading for me to come back and apologizing in advance if my dad was too harsh. She said she'd meet me in the driveway and I wouldn't have to talk to Dad if I didn't want to. She said she'd be out there, waiting, until I came home. Added that she promised not to be angry, just that I should come home as soon as I could bring myself to. It nearly broke my heart, the idea of her with both daughters missing, promising to censor her feelings if I'd just return.

Detective Alcaraz, however, was *not* breaking my heart. "I wanted to check in with you after our conversation yesterday. You've already got two calls on this phone from me. Not responding to us can be considered obstructing justice, so I need you to get back to me today. I came by your house, and you weren't home, even though school is out for the day and your father told me you didn't have any after-school activities. Please don't make me pull an officer off the streets just because you won't call me back. Look, I have a few questions to ask you about persons potentially connected to Mr. Andrews's death, and at this point I'm still politely asking for your assistance. But on the subject of your sister I couldn't possibly be more emphatic: Time is running out. Get her to bring herself in, and she'll avoid the harshest punishments. But if she remains at large, her future gets grimmer and grimmer. She wouldn't be out of prison until she was an old woman. Listen, Abby, if we find you had *any* information that you didn't share with us, you, too, could face imprisonment. I trust you understand the enormity of what I'm telling you."

Jesus. He was full-on threatening me.

But he could call me a hundred more times. There was no way I was turning in my sister. I didn't know where she was, but I wouldn't give the police even what paltry information I had on her. Not when staying on the run was her only hope.

It was a cloudless night, and under the moonlight Brian's mobile home park became actually beautiful, white from the sky and yellow from the street lamps illuminating those perfect boxes, so much neater and simpler than ordinary homes. I rumbled over gravel, stopped a hundred feet shy of Brian's, and put my car in Park.

I paused every few feet as I crept to his door, watching for a light to come on, but there was nothing. His trailer lay in the darkness, still and quiet. There was a glow from his parents' place up the hill, but if I kept to the far slope they wouldn't be able to see me even if they got up from the TV.

Just as Brian had promised, a rusty key was in the urn. I slowly turned it in the lock, my dread deepening as each tumbler clinked.

The entire mobile home creaked as I moved through it — I hadn't noticed the ricketiness when I'd been with Brian, but in my nervous state the whole structure felt like it might betray me, alerting the Andrewses to my presence or just tumbling off into the night.

I knew that Brian had told me about the key so I'd come to see him. But he'd also given me access to what was left of Jefferson's world. I could do a full-on search now, find some real evidence that would lead me to a suspect.

I didn't dare turn on a light, so I had to creep down the hallway with outstretched hands. I felt the plastic tape first and ducked beneath it. Jefferson's room got enough moonlight through the window that everything in it was outlined.

I'd been able to get to the laptop when I came in with Brian, but now I could get into the desk drawers themselves. I knew Jefferson kept a token from every girl he'd been with — a piece of underwear, a car key, an earring. It was in a shoe box; Rachael McHenry had once told me about it.

I plucked a tissue from a box on Jefferson's desk and slid open the drawers.

The top drawer contained neat rows of pencils and pens, the second, scraps of paper. The third was the size of a filing cabinet, and there were files inside — empty, but beneath them was an age-softened VANS box. I opened it and found the evidence of Jefferson's conquests. There were velvety things and scraps of fabric, as well as pins and ticket stubs. I looked for anything I recognized. There, at the bottom, was a silver chain bracelet, its clasp broken. Aha. I pocketed it and returned the box. I did a quick glance around, but there was nothing else left for me in the room.

I passed down the hall to Brian's room. I'd be waiting for him, like we'd planned. The bracelet was hidden away in my pocket. There was no way he'd know that I'd taken it. But still, I was nervous. I fidgeted as I sat on his bed, got up and paced the room. His weapons — two swords and a mace, a club with a metal end — were mounted high on the ceiling. I looked around the room, checking out the cheesy mall-goth glow-in-the-dark skulls and fairy incense burners. Underneath a particularly large specimen with glass balls for eyes were papers. Drawings. I'd figured Brian was good — in that geek fantasy, dragons-and-centaurs way — but these were incredible. I pulled them from underneath and held them up to the stray streetlight. On top was some guy in a Viking helmet. It was done in thick pencil, but the whites of his eyes were pure, brilliant, unmarred by erasures or insecurities. Next was some short guy with a lute, the tendons of the backs of his hands tender and exact. I kept flipping through.

Beneath those drawings were some of Jefferson.

Being killed.

In many different ways. Pleading before a disembodied club. Holding his throat, poisoned. Wearing a circlet in his hair like in a mythological painting, arrows piercing his torso. Placing a revolver into his own throat. The details were what made the drawings most alarming. In each one, Jefferson was wearing a pair of jeans I remembered well, rips over the knees and a name brand stitched across the back pocket. He deflected a blow with just the expression he would have taken on should his brother have struck him, outrage and fury and surprise exploding on his face.

Holy crap. Brian was way more messed up than I'd thought.

I grabbed as many drawings as I could clench in one hand and headed into the hallway.

I wondered: How much *had* Brian hated Jefferson? Before, his lack of grief over the death, his unwillingness to put on a false face, was almost refreshing. Now it seemed like more than rebellion. It seemed genuinely cold and uncaring.

Like a killer.

21.

shoved the drawings into my bag as I slammed out of the trailer — and I got them out of view just in time, because before I could get to my car the door to Brian's parents' trailer opened. Mrs. Andrews stood in the light and stared in my direction. "Hello?" she called. "Who's there?"

I could have bolted for my car. But she would've had a good view of it as I drove off. She'd realize who I was as soon as she put her mind to it.

"Hi, Mrs. Andrews," I called, "I was just trying to find Brian. Is he home?"

"No," she called, her arms crossed. "He's at youth symphony."

"Right, of course. Okay. Thanks, anyway!"

"Abby Goodwin?" she called.

"Yeah, it's me."

"Come talk to me for a moment. I'd really like to speak to you."

Fear dropped my arms to my sides. "I don't know. My parents are expecting me back." That was dumb. She already thought I was coming to see Brian — I couldn't exactly claim that my parents were expecting me home right away. I'd have to give up. "Okay, sure, no prob."

Mrs. Andrews held the door open for me. She had one of

those entirely unextraordinary faces, blank and trusting. Firm, glittery eyeballs behind thick glasses. "Thanks, Abby, come in."

She sat me at a kitchen barstool and served me a cookie on a napkin. Dry knobs of chocolate rolled off the top and pinged on the floor. It was one old cookie . . . a cookie, I realized, that had been made well before Jefferson died. I ceremonially broke it in half but couldn't bring myself to eat it.

"I didn't realize you were friends with Brian," she said. "I'd always thought of you as closer to Jefferson."

"Jefferson and I weren't too close. Same year in school. I'm sorry about your loss, Mrs. Andrews."

"Jill. And thank you." Her words had no color. "But you're Maya's sister, of course. So you would have spent plenty of time with Jefferson one way or another, right? When he came over to tutor her? How is Maya?"

"I don't really know."

"I want you to know I don't think it's true. That she —" She closed her eyes and mustered up some internal strength. I could almost hear the wheeze of tears peaking and subsiding somewhere just beyond where her voice began. "— killed Jefferson. Doug wanted to get a restraining order after it was clear she'd become obsessed. But I told him she was just a teen girl. We've all had deep crushes that are close to craziness, right? I hope I wasn't wrong. Jefferson seemed to invite feelings like that from young ladies."

"You weren't wrong," I said emphatically.

"He was really a remarkable young man. I'm not saying that just as his mother. The stories I could tell you about him." She looked like she was about to totally lose it, but she cleared her throat. "Doug said he found you with Brian last night," she said.

"Is he home right now, your husband?" I said, my fear suddenly doubling.

"He's in bed. Tell me, have you found anything unusual about Brian while you were spending time with him?"

"No. Not at all."

"Really, nothing unusual at all, even though he just lost his brother?"

"Well, yeah, of course he seems depressed and different because of that," I said, trying to sound convincing.

"Have you ever been at all . . . curious about him?"

"I don't get what you mean," I said, crumbling half of the cookie between my fingers before I realized what I was doing.

"I never have any idea what he's thinking. Now less than ever. He's a complicated boy."

I leaned forward. I couldn't come right out and say, *Do you think Brian killed his brother?* So instead I asked, "Are you wondering whether he . . . did something wrong?"

She sat and glittered at me for a moment. "No," she sighed. "I'm just wondering whether he might know something that he hasn't told me."

I debated how to answer. "He had a lot of negative feelings about Jefferson. I bet you know that."

"Not really. I know they're very different boys."

It was unnerving and sad, telling a mother about her sons' lives. "I'd try to keep your son out of everyone's attention, Mrs. Andrews," I said. "He's not the grieving sibling most people would expect. It could be a little shocking."

"Okay," she said. Obviously, I hadn't given the kind of answer she'd been expecting. What had she wanted, unconditional sympathy, faked understanding? A stumbling confession about my sister? Maybe she herself didn't know. Either way, I'd wounded her deeply. Or just revealed the wounds aching under the surface. The bruised skin beneath her eyes rippled and the lines around her mouth fell even more vertically.

"You mentioned other girls being crazy about him?" I asked, hoping I might be able to learn something.

Mrs. Andrews sighed. "He was on his phone all the time. Some would call our line if he wasn't picking up his. His father didn't like that, I can tell you. But it was nice he had so many people that liked him. We never had to worry about him being a loner." (Left unsaid: *Unlike Brian.*)

"Did you ever talk to Caitlin?" I asked, fishing.

She shook her head. "I don't remember that name."

"Cheyenne?"

"Oh, she was the smart one, wasn't she? I liked talking to her whenever she'd call. Very polite."

"And Rose was over here, after?"

"Yes. Rose was a big help. That poor girl. She truly loved him. But then again, you all loved him, didn't you?"

"Everybody loved him," I said. Because it was the easy thing to say.

"Look," Mrs. Andrews said, eyeing the clock, "I won't keep you any longer."

"'Night," I said. "Tell Brian I stopped by, okay?"

"I will."

As I left, I thought about the pictures in my bag. Jefferson, crisscrossed by half a dozen knives, his head parted by an ax. Then I thought about Mrs. Andrews, alone in a dim kitchen, cleaning up the bits of cookie I had nervously sprayed all over her floor.

22.

As promised, my mom was waiting for me in the driveway. She was dressed in old sweatpants that had permanent wrinkles around the knees and was reading a drugstore romance beneath the motion sensor light, waving her hand whenever it shut off. She jumped to her feet as I pulled into the driveway. It was nearly nine.

"I'm sorry, Mom," I said before I'd even gotten out of my car.

"It's okay, honey," she said, hugging me as soon as I was near enough. I could feel her soft breath at the base of my hairline. Cody leaped against us. "Thank goodness you came home."

"Of course I came home. Of course."

"This has been so hard for you, I know. I'm so desperately sorry that you have to go through all of this. I don't know if I've said that well enough yet. With one daughter missing, it's too easy to neglect the one who's left." Perhaps for comfort, she was wearing a Christmas sweater, the same one she was wearing in the big family picture in the hallway, clutching a baby Maya. It was giving off a damp wool smell under the humidity of her tears.

"You, too, Mom," I said. "Is Dad pissed?"

She laughed a little. "You could say that. But don't worry about him. He'll be better by morning."

"I don't want to have to talk to the police again," I said.

"Shh," she said. "You shouldn't have sent us from the room, then. Why did you do that? But, shh, not to worry now. Maya will be back and this will all be cleared up. Life will be back to normal soon, you'll see."

"I hope so," I said, shuddering.

"Where were you, just now?" she asked.

I told her about Cheyenne, how we'd had a fight yesterday (I said it was because of the pressure we were all under, and my mother apparently didn't see the need to ask for any details), and how I'd spent the day with Brian and met his parents. By bringing them up I staved off any questions about what I'd actually been up to tonight.

"His mother must be an absolute wreck," my mom said.

"Not really," I said. "I mean, yes, of course she is, but she's also able to do everyday things. She gave me a cookie. It was totally stale, but still. It's not like she's bawling all the time."

"It's just so sad," my mom said. "Times like this make you realize that life is so precious, you know?"

I nodded into her shoulder. I did know. I thought. It was hard to tell when there was just so much strategizing around maintaining life. It wasn't some gooey wonder zone. Life recently seemed to be just jockeying and positioning, vowing and lying.

"She asked me if I was ever suspicious of Brian," I said.

My mom held me at arm's length. "What did you tell her?"

"That he didn't ever have much good to say about his brother. Everyone knows that. But there was something I didn't show her. Something I found in Brian's room."

"What? Tell me anything you know. Immediately. Even the most minor detail can turn out to be very important, honey."

"Okay, okay! I am."

I pulled Brian's sketches out of my bag and handed them to my mother. I hadn't planned to do it. But I couldn't hold it in. I wanted my mother to decide what to do.

She examined them right then and there. When the motion sensor light clicked off I waved at it so she could continue uninterrupted.

"They're pretty vivid, huh?" I said. "He's a really good artist."

"Unfortunately for him," Mom said. "If he weren't, someone could argue that this guy in the picture wasn't Jefferson. But this is definitely him."

"Brian's not *killing him* in any of them," I protested weakly. "It's just that Jefferson happens to be dying."

"Honey," Mom said, "you did the right thing to show these to me." She sounded relieved, but there was something else there, an emotion I'd never detected in her before. The opposite of relief: a gearing up. Something like bloodlust. Not a motherly feeling. What had I done?

When we went inside my dad was pacing and waiting to lay into me but she took the heat, yelling back at him while I slinked upstairs with Cody. The yells soon subsided, and I could hear frantic whispering. She was telling him about the drawings. Then it was quiet as doom down there.

When my mom took me to school the next morning, she slowed down and we peered through the trees as we passed Brian's mobile home complex.

A police cruiser was at the Andrewses' door.

THURSDAY, MAY 16

23.

From Brian's place all the way to school, the traffic was terrible. My paranoid imagination attached the congestion to Brian's arrest, somehow, that it was already on all the morning radio shows and people were so shocked that they lost control of their cars, that the astonishment of my betraying Brian had caused thousands of commuters to fall out of their normal patterns and trip over themselves and wonder *Who's the bitch who betrayed that sweet, sweet kid?*

After I said good-bye to my mom, I headed straight for my locker. I already had the books I needed, but I craved the solitary ritual of it, pretending that finals and APs were all I had to be worried about. I couldn't help but see Brian's locker as I passed. The lock was gone, replaced by a loop of tough plastic. That was always the sign that someone had gotten into major trouble. *Nate's been expelled, they looped his locker. Marisa's back in the hospital, they looped her locker. Brian's in police custody because of Abby Goodwin, they looped his locker.*

Where did kids who skipped classes but still wanted to stay in the school building hang out? It was weird that I didn't know, but I'd never been friends with those sorts of kids. The auditorium was drama territory; the shed by the bus circle was for smokers. I couldn't just join in with any of them. So I sat in the bathroom instead.

When the passing period bell rang, I waited near Cheyenne's classroom. I followed her to her locker and put my hands over her eyes. It was our usual trick; normally she'd shriek my name, but today she shrieked terrified nonsense instead. "Abby? What the hell are you doing?" she said once she'd calmed down.

"What do you mean, 'what am I doing?'"

"You scared me. You weren't in psych, so I figured you weren't coming in today."

"Nope," I said. I was going to apologize, but I bit my tongue. I didn't really need a reason for my actions, did I? Not these days.

"I figured you were avoiding me," she said, slamming a book into her locker, picking it back out, and slamming it back in.

"Oh no," I said, figuring I was experiencing a wave of garden variety Cheyenne insecurity, "of course not."

"I don't think it's an 'of course not' kind of situation."

"What are you talking about?"

"'Congrats on the Florida's Scholars, Cheyenne; hey, good job, Cheyenne. Gee, thanks, everybody, who'd you find out from?'"

"I didn't tell anyone," I lied. I'd find out some way to tell her the truth later, I promised myself.

"Someone did, because the word's out. And I only told *you*."

"I don't know what to tell you." I'd never lied to Cheyenne before this week. Not about anything major, at least. But all

176

rules were off since Jefferson was killed. I'd make it up to her once things were back to normal.

"Everyone's looking at me weird," she said. "It's real fun to be me these days, let me tell ya."

"Tell me about it — I get it," I said, relieved to say something unabashedly true to my best friend. "I'm sorry."

"Come to calc with me, at least," Cheyenne said.

I shook my head. "I haven't done any homework for ages."

She clutched my arm and adopted a mock parental tone. "You, missy, are coming with me."

I let her lead me to the math wing. I was about to ask her if she'd heard any rumors about Brian when we passed someone who stopped me in my tracks. Rose Nelson.

Rose stopped Cheyenne in her tracks, too. And Cheyenne and I stopped Rose in her tracks. It was like some god somewhere had pressed Pause. Cheyenne finally broke the silence. "Hey, Rose."

"Hey, Rose," I parroted.

Rose Nelson stared back.

"Come on, let's get going," Cheyenne said.

"How's your sister, Abby?" Rose asked. She was beaming like a fluorescent light, her books clasped tight and demure against her chest. It was warmth and chilliness at the same time.

"Screw you," I said.

"No," Rose said, "screw *you*," and she hurled her books at me. I'd always thought that only boys really got violent, that girls lashed out by excluding one another, but times must have changed. Most of her books missed. Unfortunately for me she was coming from calculus, though, and the honors book is college level and really fat and contains an extra two hundred pages on multivariable derivatives and is brand-new with sharp corners. She got me square on the shoulder, and it really hurt. I picked up the book and threw it back, ripping the cover off in the process. I got her elbow. Then Cheyenne joined in, picking the book back up and lobbing it at Rose. It missed and slapped loudly against the wall. By now everyone in the hallway was watching.

"Come on, Abby, let's *go*," Cheyenne said.

"It wasn't *Brian Andrews*," Rose said. "Please. We know exactly who killed Jefferson. And her name is Maya Goodwin."

"Whatever," I said. "Just because you couldn't keep your man in your bed doesn't mean my sister had anything to do with it."

As far as comebacks go, it was pretty lame, but tears immediately stood in Rose's eyes. "How could you say that to me? My boyfriend is *dead*." Rose's friends, and unfortunately there were always dozens of them around, started swarming over. They circled her and looked at me reproachfully. This was going nowhere fast. I let Cheyenne lead me away.

"Good one, Abby," Cheyenne muttered as we sped to calc. "What is *wrong* with us?"

"I don't know," I said, sliding into my seat. I felt both sullen and energized.

There was a quiz, but I said I didn't feel well and got out of it. I toyed with my phone under the desk instead. I'd gotten a message from Keith: call asap. business stuff. urgent. Maybe I would call him. But not anytime soon. What I didn't need at all right now were even more complications.

What I *did* need, though, was to find out exactly what was happening with Brian. I dreaded finding out, even as I wanted it more than anything.

I excused myself to the bathroom and called the Andrewses' home line from a stall. I had the number keyed in under Jefferson's name; it felt unholy pressing Send. Brian's dad answered. "Hello?"

"Mr. Andrews?"

"Yes. Who is this?"

"Abby. Abby Goodwin."

"Brian can't talk to you."

"I'm sorry, I . . . I just want to know if he's okay."

"Did you hear me?" he asked, his voice rising. "I said he can't talk to you. Don't call here."

"Does he not want to talk to me or *can't* he? Has he been arrested, Mr. Andrews?"

The line went dead. I stared at my phone. I heard the sizzle of a dunked cigarette in the next stall, followed by a toilet flushing. Did Brian hate me? Or was he arrested? There was no way I'd find out, not for a while. I went back to math class in a stupor.

Maybe the lives of both the Andrews boys were over now.

FRIDAY, MAY 17

24.

My parents kept saying it was a good idea for me to go to school, but each time I went it worked out pretty much like I predicted — that is, horribly. That night I closed myself in my room and spent a few cathartic hours on the phone. First I tried Maya, but of course there was no answer. So instead I spent the evening talking to Cheyenne. I got her to agree to skip the first half of the next day and go to the mall with me. Our plan worked fine until my mom went to get her hair done at Salon la Floride and found me and Chantal chatting at the highlighting station. She started yanking out foil, had the assistant rinse out my hair, marched me out of the mall, and insisted on delivering me to school in person. (With, I might add, some crazy-looking hair.)

My heart started fluttering as we approached Xavier High. I couldn't put together a coherent argument for why I couldn't go into school, nothing that my mom would buy; my protests sprayed out, like juice from a bludgeoned fruit. "I don't want to go. I really can't. By tomorrow I'll be better, I promise. But I can't today. I'm tired; I can't face everyone. They're going to think I'm ugly and crazy and guilty and they're going to ask me all over again about Maya and

Jefferson and Brian and it's just horrendous so don't make me go in."

What was the precise reason for my anxiety? Plain old nerves, maybe. My father had made the police promise not to reveal the source of the pictures, but I still felt like my nasty secret was written on my face, and it was only a matter of time until someone noticed it.

At one point my huddling against the car door freaked out my mom enough that she pulled over. Between us, resting on top of the parking brake, was a wax bag containing two toasted coconut donuts and a vanilla iced coffee. My mom knew my favorite comfort food and had stopped by a drive-through on the way. She'd gotten over her anger and was back to being wonderful. But I couldn't figure out how to make her see the scale of the torment in my mind. It zapped me whenever my thoughts left perfect center, like an electrified floor surrounding a mouse.

"What *is* it, Abby? Is this about Brian?"

"It's not just Brian. I can handle people one-on-one, but I can't stand to find out what specific little nasty things people have to say about Jefferson and Maya and me and Brian and all of it, you know?"

Mom rested her head against the leather steering wheel cover. "I think you're traumatized by the fact that your sister's still missing, and you're finding it hard to put your anguish into words. But you have to let life get back to some semblance of normality."

"Mom! I think this counts as extenuating circumstances.

Maya's *missing*." I'd heard her tell my dad last night that she hadn't been able to do any cleaning or cooking and that they'd have to hire a maid until their little girl returned. If my mom wasn't letting her own life return to normal, why should I be expected to? But she was definitely right that the way things were now couldn't continue for much longer.

"It's already Friday; the weekend will be here before you know it. Returning to school will be like diving into a cold pool. It'll be fine once you start swimming. Just get in, already." She seemed very satisfied with that metaphor. She continued to repeat it. Her red bangs shivered every time she did.

"Fine," I said.

"You have plenty of great friends looking out for you. Today's going to be easier than you think. I'll pick you up after and we can get manicures."

I nestled the donuts and coffee into my schoolbag. "What you can do is make an appointment so I can get this horrendous half dye job fixed. But later. I'll get a ride after school. Thanks, Mom."

"I love you."

"I love you, too."

Madame Rutman was both mournful and ecstatic when I showed up halfway through French. *"Bonjour, Abigail! Classe, levez-vous! Répétez, s'il vous plaît: 'Bonjour, Abigail!'"*

After my riotous reintroduction, I slinked to my seat, kept my head low, and did my best to concentrate on subjunctive conjugations. I've never written down more and understood less. When the bell finally rang, I was the first out, and hovered in a dark spot at the end of the hallway, where Cheyenne had fourth-period Spanish. I glanced through the window. They were finishing a quiz, and of course she was working on it overtime.

While I was waiting, Rose came whizzing out of a nearby door. She nearly crashed into me. "Oh," she said, checking me out as I hovered in the darkness, "that's creepy."

"I'm waiting for Cheyenne."

"I'm sure you are. You guys should really work on expanding your circle of friends. Was she helping Brian, too?"

I did a mental inventory of the books in my hand. French workbooks were way too light to bother throwing — why couldn't I have had fourth-period history? "You're freaking obsessive, you know that?" I said.

"There sure are a ton of obsessives around, aren't there? Like your sister. I'm wondering if she and her goth boy hatched some plan. Everyone's saying he killed his brother with one of those creepy weapons on his wall. That he drew hundreds of pictures of it. But wouldn't he need help? If Maya didn't do the deed, then maybe she held his dagger for him or something."

"Brian's not goth. He's not even emo." What exactly was I trying to accomplish with *that* line of argument? I've always been terrible at fighting. I tried again. "You're pointing a lot of fingers. Getting pretty loud. Accusing everyone in sight except for one person."

Her eyes narrowed. "Who, you?"

"No. You."

Her eyes filled with tears, and I watched her expert transition from bitch to victim. It was really amazing. "You monster," she said softly, looking around for someone to rescue her. But we were at the end of the hallway. There was no one.

The door to the Spanish classroom opened and Cheyenne barreled out. "Abby!"

"Hey."

"Hey, Rose!" Cheyenne said, making a fist.

Rose turned martyr and fled down the hall.

We watched her run, flip-flops kicking out awkwardly. "She's really fragile, you know," Cheyenne said drily. "We should be more careful with her."

I nodded. "Yep. But let me tell you, it was fun while it lasted. Wanna pretend we don't have any classes fifth or sixth period?"

"You got it. Rocking highlights, by the way."

We started toward the front doors. I pointed at the hallway clock dramatically as we passed under. "Eleven-thirty on Friday. Know what that means?"

"Wait, don't tell me." Cheyenne stayed quiet for a long time. She hated when she couldn't meet a challenge. "Damn. I have no idea."

"Sixty-seven hours exactly since I talked to the cops. Deadline's almost up. The search for Maya's about to go federal."

"Sounds heavy," Cheyenne said. "But I don't know what that means. What do the federal police do differently?"

I paused. Actually, I didn't really know. Now that Brian was everyone's favorite suspect, would there still be warrants and unannounced visits and total chaos for my family? Or had my giving those drawings to my mom gotten Maya off the hook? Even if that was true, I shuddered to think about the costs. I'd betrayed Brian. But I couldn't bring myself to voice any of that to Cheyenne. "What it does mean," I said, "is that I start ducking every time I see a police car."

"You," Cheyenne said, "have turned into a bad, bad girl."

She was joking. But it was so not funny.

A vice principal was posted by the front entrance to catch skippers, but he smiled at us and held open the door. No way sweet girls like Abby and Cheyenne would be truants. We waved and walked outside. As soon as we did, though, I saw a certain car in the front lot and froze.

It wasn't a cop car. But it was the one thing that could make me pray for cops.

Keith and Blake were lounging against an old Cadillac, smoking and watching the school entrance. I remembered Keith's text message from yesterday, how he'd demanded to see me, how I'd blown it off. They leaped to their feet as soon as we stepped out of the doors. I watched Blake's hand go to an inside pocket of her leather jacket and start to pull something out.

"Whoa," Cheyenne said, "isn't that . . . ?"

"Yes," I said. "Back into the school. Now."

Once we were back inside, the vice principal nearby, my heart rate slowed. "Okay," I said. "We're going out the back way, by the driver's ed course."

"What do they want with us?" Cheyenne asked as we power walked.

"No idea. You want to go find out?"

We exited through the back entrance, stood in the shadow of a balcony, and scanned for Blake and Keith. Nothing, until . . . "They're over there," Cheyenne whispered. And sure enough, the same old Cadillac pulled up at the other side of the barbed-wire fence. Keith and Blake watched us through the window. "What do we do?" Cheyenne asked.

"We run."

I immediately took off across the field, Cheyenne yelping and running to catch up to me. I risked a look over at the car and saw Blake climbing the fence. But Keith pulled her back to the far side. I held out a hand for Cheyenne to stop.

Keith and Blake yelled something at us that I couldn't make out. Finally, they threw up their arms in disgust, got in the car, and sped away.

"What was *that* about?" Cheyenne asked.

"I'm glad not to know, I think."

"Me, too," Cheyenne said, looping her arm through mine. We wandered off, alert to any signs of Blake and Keith, and wound up at Ernie's cavernous gas station. We sat out of view around back and wolfed down the donuts my mom had bought me, which by now had greased through their waxed paper bag. "Rose is totally hysterical, isn't she? I mean that in the crazy way, not the funny way. Bitch needs to center."

"She *did* just lose her boyfriend," I pointed out.

"Sure, Abby, that makes sense, hurl textbooks at the girl and then defend her later. I *knew* it wasn't Maya, by the way."

"You did not!" I said, indignant. "You were the most suspicious thing ever."

"Oh, please. I was being *emotionally pragmatic*, sure, about the *reality* of the *situation*, but I never *really* believed it." She took in a gaping mouthful of donut and waited for the gummy clot to clear her throat. "When's Maya coming back?"

"I don't know if she knows Brian's the prime suspect," I said. "I haven't been able to reach her recently."

"Have you tried everything?"

I nodded.

"Did you know that Jefferson messed around with Donna Meadows, too?" Cheyenne continued. "Same story as usual. Flowers and romance and pledges of devotion, and then the sudden cruel drop. That was back when they were freshmen. Somehow she kept it quiet all this time. Embarrassed to be part of the trend, I guess."

I knew all about Donna Meadows and didn't feel like chatting about Jefferson. But I could sense how much Cheyenne wanted to talk, so I barreled in: "Drug dealer, sociopath, brother destroyer, valedictorian blackmailer, all-around punk. Do you think he got away with it all just because he was so hot? Remember that picture you took at the beach for Rebecca's bat mitzvah? That was eighth grade — he was just *fourteen*. And damn. You could see those three old ladies in the background, staring at his back muscles. They bought him a beer. A beer!" I had started getting nervous — Cheyenne was staring at me something heavy.

"What do you mean, 'valedictorian blackmailer'?" she asked.

I shrugged. "Brian told me. Don't worry about it. Your secret's safe with me."

"You mean, you're believing the guy who killed his own brother over your best friend?"

"No. Who cares? You don't even know what he told me, anyway."

"I can just imagine what Brian Andrews would have told you, Abby."

"You're not mad at me, are you? Why are you mad at me?"

"I'm not," she said, ticked.

"Don't *worry* about it. Please."

"I know. I'm not trying to say Jeff wasn't a total ass to me.

I'm jittery these days, that's all. There's enough going on without people spreading extra crap about me."

"Look," I said, sighing, "I know you didn't *kill* him. Let's move on. You got your BlackBerry? I want to see if Maya's online."

Cheyenne handed it to me. Maya wasn't online, so I sent her a Facebook message. I left it a bit vague, in case the police were monitoring somehow.

To: Maya Goodwin

From: Abby Goodwin

Hey. What's going on? Dumb question. A lot, huh? I hope you're hidden somewhere good. What are you doing with yourself? Watching a lot of TV? Getting panicky all the time? I am, just worrying about you. I'm keeping Mom and Dad in order (they seem pretty fine, actually, considering you're missing and all. I mean they miss you, of course, but it's not like they're TOTALLY falling apart. Not COMPLETELY). Anyway, the big news is that Brian's all but the confirmed killer. I know, killed his own brother. At least that's what everyone's saying. Look, you were the only person there that night who's still alive. Now that Brian's in custody, people are a whole lot more likely to believe you. If you know that you didn't kill him, then come back! The truth will wash itself out.

I miss you. You know what's real and what's not so what are you afraid of? I get that this is a total 180, but everything's changed now that Brian's caught.

The phone beeped, and I passed it to Cheyenne. "What does that mean?"

"Low battery. You've got a little while, but you'd better finish up."

"Okay."

Cheyenne headed around to the station's front door. "I need more donuts. But we're at Ernie's, so year-old Entenmann's will have to cut it. Want anything?"

"Get me some of those little powdered ones. Let me hold on to your phone, though. I want to see if Maya tries to IM. Maybe she only logs on during the day or something."

"That's a stretch," Cheyenne said, "but fine. See you in a sec."

Ugh. More donuts. But eating bad made me feel good. I worked my hand under my shirt, running my fingertips along the side of my abdomen. I used to do that all the time, until Cheyenne basically staged an intervention about it. It's not like I've ever had an eating disorder; I just like to check whether I feel muscle or cool, limp fat. I'd thought no one noticed me doing it. But Cheyenne had, so I try to abstain when she's around.

The phone pinged. It was a message from Maya.

To: Abby Goodwin
From: Maya Goodwin
Really? They think brian did it? That sucks, actually. You wrote it like I should be all overjoyed. Honestly I cant believe

that he DID it. He didn't love Jefferson, that's for sure, but he wasnt about to kill him, either.

But at the same time I cant stay here much longer. Im so bored and my life is on hold and I cant contact anyone. V's set me up with money and stuff, but im still dying here. How about I slowly come back, one person at a time. We can start with you. Coffee?

To: Maya Goodwin
From: Abby Goodwin
Call me. From a pay phone.

I sent the message and pulled out my own phone, waiting for the blank screen to light and tell me where my life was heading next.

Soon enough, a message came through . . . but not the one I'd expected.

Cheyenne arrived with a huge soda and a bag of donuts. She handed me the donuts, but I waved them away. "We have to go," I said, staring at the message. "And no bailing out on this one."

25

He's *what*?" Cheyenne asked.

"He's not in custody," I said flatly.

"Of course he's in custody. He basically drew himself killing Jefferson. His own *parents* think he killed him. It doesn't take a brainiac to know he's the one."

"I don't know what to tell you. I'm not making this up. He wants to see me once school's out." I showed her the text message.

"You're not actually going to see him, are you?"

"Don't for a second think that I *want* to. But I should at least find out what he knows." Of course I wasn't really expecting Brian to confess to me or anything — but if there was any chance of him giving me info, I had to try to get him to do it. I could also see what I could do about relieving the guilt about sounding the alarm on him.

"I'm not surprised at all," Cheyenne said. "He's got a puppy crush on you. And it's only gotten stronger the more desperate he gets. Who else can he turn to, after all?" She was right. It was an unfairness of the world, that I could be the top of Brian's friend list, when he would barely crack the top thirty of mine. Under ordinary circumstances. "Don't you think it could be dangerous to see him?" she asked.

"Dangerous? No. He's not some psychopath. He might

have killed his brother, but he had a reason to. He doesn't have any reason to kill me. Or you."

"I know he doesn't have a reason to kill *me*," Cheyenne said, "but I'm not so sure about you, Li'l Miss Amateur Detective."

"Cheyenne! Oh my god! He *likes* me," I said stubbornly.

"Off we go, then," Cheyenne said, sighing. "But we're picking up baseball bats from my garage first."

"Really?" I said, rolling my eyes. Then I remembered Brian's drawings. "Fine. We'll pick up baseball bats."

It was all I could do to make Cheyenne leave the bats in the car. What an image we would have made, two chicks stalking across the grass with weapons in hand, like from a gangster movie with really bad casting.

Brian asked me to meet him in a stubbly weedy area under a highway bridge, one of the county's token attempts at a park. He was sitting cross-legged on top of a picnic table, staring at a heron stalking in the reeds at the water's edge. An unbroken plume of smoke rose as he sucked his way through a pack of cigarettes.

"Do you see any guns on him? Magical crossbows?" Cheyenne whispered.

"Stop," I said.

When Brian saw us he stubbed out his cigarette. He was wearing a heavy plaid shirt, even though it was a warm day. His eyes were bloodshot and rimmed in red.

"What is she doing here?" he asked, pointing his smoldering stub at Cheyenne.

"Good to see you, too, Brian," she said cracklingly.

"I said to come alone, Abby," he said sullenly. "I wasn't kidding."

"You can probably see why I might not want to go alone to secluded parks these days," I said. "No offense."

"Why don't you guys have a seat?" he offered.

Cheyenne and I sat on the bench. Brian scooted to the end of the tabletop so he wouldn't be breathing right on top of us. Cheyenne crossed her arms and sort of leaned away. She'd evidently decided her official role was to be silent chaperone. I was glad for it, that Brian and I could talk without feeling obligated to keep including her.

"What was it like, the police questioning?" I asked.

"Worse that it was for you, I bet," he said. "They came by my house at five-thirty in the morning. Laid right into me."

"What did Jamison say to you? Or was it Alcaraz?"

"Got their names memorized, eh? It was Jamison. At first he said that he just wanted to talk to me. Then he said the police had received some drawings of mine, of my brother. Any idea how they got those, Abby?"

I shook my head.

He shuddered. "My mom was there, and *she* knew about the drawings, too. But she said nothing I'd drawn had ever left the house. She claimed she found them cleaning up my room. It was all some really complicated power game — she was probably the one to inform the police, right? Who else would have found them?"

He was probing, trying to see if I'd confess to turning in the drawings. Which meant he wasn't sure that it was me. I dug in my heels. "Your own mother. Man."

"I don't know it was her. I don't think she believes I did it. I think she's just really messed up and really confused and looking to anyone to provide some answers. Anyway, Jamison started asking me the exact things you'd expect police to ask, like where I'd been the night my brother died." His face had turned blotchy, and his eyes looked both shriveled and shiny, like beetle shells. "They'd never bothered to ask that before."

"Oh," I said. I hadn't thought to ask, either. Duh. "What did you tell him?"

"I was home playing a video game," he said. "Luckily, I'd used a different save game slot. I showed him the time stamp. He asked me not to boot up the machine anymore, that it could be useful evidence."

So Brian had an alibi. Sort of. I had no idea how a court would treat that kind of thing. My mind raced — had I been too hasty telling Maya she could come back? "So that," I said, "means that you couldn't have done it."

"I'm not sure how convincing video game evidence is," he said, with a hint of a smile.

"Yeah, totally," I said, trying to tease out more of the smile. "Unless, of course, you literally had a jury of your peers."

"Do you know that whoever it was hit Jefferson at least nine times? Split his forehead so deep that the bone was showing? The police showed me pictures. They think it was a rock."

"How'd they look? Did you get it right in your drawings?" Cheyenne asked.

He refused to look at her. "In any case, the case against me isn't as convincing as, say, proof that someone had written a ton of love notes that had never been answered, had left a rose in Jefferson's bed, then dug it out of the trash when he threw it out, painted the thorns gold, and placed it in his locker. That kind of thing would be much more convincing."

"You don't have proof that Maya did any of those things," Cheyenne said. "So be careful what you're saying, little man."

"Are you so sure I'm talking about Maya?" he said, staring at me.

"We're not sure *who* you're talking about," I said. "Tell us."

"Jefferson might have dicked me around," Brian said, "but he also talked to me, especially when no one else was around. And all I'm going to say is that he didn't give a shit about *any* of the girls he was messing around with. Not a single one. Not Maya. Not Rose. Not either of you."

"Either of us?" Cheyenne laughed. "Who do you think you're kidding, little boy?"

"Seriously. You've got some serious confusion going on,"

I said. I could see what he was doing. He was miserable, suspected I'd betrayed him, and was trying to hurt Cheyenne and me by lumping us in with the rest of Jefferson's girls. Making it out that I was chasing after Jefferson in death the same way all the other girls chased after him in life. "Making shit up isn't going to get you anywhere," I warned. "Do you realize how few allies you have right now? You want to burn through some more? Or do you want me to start bringing up the money you owe your brother? *Owed* your brother?"

He looked at me with hollow eyes, then sighed. "I take it back."

"I know you're desperate, but that was way too far," I continued. I held my breath, scared he'd start spouting again.

I stood up to leave, and so did Cheyenne. We made it ten paces before he started freaking out. "I'm sorry," Brian said again. "Don't leave yet. I don't know what I'm doing. This whole thing is making me so paranoid."

"What you can do is think about the crap you just pulled and get your facts straight in your head," Cheyenne said, wrapping her arms tightly around her torso. "You little weirdo."

"Leave him alone," I said. I crossed back over to Brian, tousled his hair. "I'll catch you soon, okay?"

He hid his head under his shirt, like a spooked bird. "I didn't do it," he said.

"Nobody's saying you did," I told him. Which I think we both knew was a lie.

"Wanting to kill him and killing him are two different things," he said.

I nodded — and didn't point out that while what he said was true, wanting to kill Jefferson was a big prerequisite to doing it.

I'd wondered if he was capable of it, and the answer was more and more clearly yes.

I realized: I'd wanted Maya's name to be cleared, sure. But not like this.

26.

"What the hell was that about?" Cheyenne said as we walked to the car. "He's seriously unhinged. I can't believe the police still let him walk around free. He's completely nuts. Completely. Nuts."

"He's not a risk to anyone," I said quietly.

"Sorry?"

"Why the police let him go. He's not a risk to anyone. They're obviously thinking he could have killed his brother, but that he couldn't possibly kill anyone else. So they let him go free while they're collecting more evidence. What good would it do anyone to lock him up?"

"Careful with your tender little judgment calls. Your life is at risk here."

My life wasn't at risk. Our encounter with Brian had left me profoundly sad. I rocked my head against the metal of the car door, took a deep breath. Brian was still at that picnic bench, his head down between his hands. Totally alone. Where would he go?

"Do you want a ride?" I called out to him.

"No way!" Cheyenne whispered urgently, trying to snag my shirt and pull me into the car. I let her try, felt her stretch my shirt while I waited for Brian to look up. I called out to him again. He did look at me briefly, then put his head back down. "See?" Cheyenne said. "He doesn't want anyone to take him anywhere. Get in."

I did. We left Brian behind.

Once Cheyenne dropped me off, I jumped into my own car and pulled onto the interstate to go to Veronica's. She was home — I knew she would be; even when life was normal, she rarely left, because she thought the cats got lonely without her — and sat me down, poured me a glass of sweet wine with the vague proclamation that it "was five o'clock somewhere." I accepted it; maybe I was twenty-one somewhere, too.

"I think I told you that you weren't supposed to be in touch with me or Maya," Veronica said brightly. "I was pretty sure we'd definitely decided that." There might have been some disapproval somewhere deep in her tone, but it was overridden by the fact that she was feeling lonely and chatty. She barely sounded pissed at all.

"Yeah," I said, "and it was probably a good idea. But now I'm worried that Maya's going to come back, anyway." I explained how focus had shifted onto Brian, that he seemed all but guilty, and that the only thing still making Maya look culpable was her very absence. That I'd told her as much, but now I'd learned that Brian had a sort-of alibi, so I wasn't at all sure I'd done the right thing.

"When you two were younger," she said, "during that year when my daughter was with your father, we went to the circus, and Maya fell in love with a stuffed toucan someone was selling from a cart. Just madly in love with it. Do you remember that?"

I did, but I didn't say anything. Why was she getting into this now?

"And we'd already spent so much money that day that your father and I said she couldn't have it. She was spitting mad, said we were monsters. She concentrated on your father, but reserved some choice words for me, too. Where an eleven-year-old learned to say stuff like that, I'll never know. When we got home, she found the toy online and showed us the page. It was a few dollars cheaper, maybe. But we still said no. Then, the next day your father found his credit card upside down in his wallet and confronted Maya. She kept saying she hadn't used it, but it was pretty clear she had when a toucan arrived in the mail. We asked you what you knew, and you said you'd been with Maya all day and she hadn't stolen the card. You thought you were being clever, but your wording was so slippery, making it clear only that *she* hadn't used the card. So I called you on it. And you fessed up right away. You'd bought the toy for her. Because you couldn't stand to see her without it. Even though you were older, and must have known that you were probably going to get caught, and that as the older sister, you should have known better and would take more blame. You knew all that, and you still did it. You couldn't stand to see her upset."

I nodded. I knew this story. But Veronica got one part wrong: I'd wanted that toucan, too. When Maya had started neglecting it, I'd transferred it to my room. "Is this supposed to prove some important lesson?"

"Honey," Veronica said, "you're throwing up defenses. Don't. It was just a revealing moment to me, said so much about the nature of your sisterhood. It's come into my mind for a reason — I think the same thing might be happening now. You don't want Maya to have to spend any more time on her own, don't want to see your parents continuing to panic. But your goodwill can actually damage her in the long run. You can get her in deeper trouble by being too good to her right now."

"I thought we were wrong to keep her away when it was safe to come home. But it's not as airtight a case against Brian as I thought." I pulled out my phone and stared at it glumly. "I need her to call me, already."

Veronica shook her head, stared out her window. The pond outside was heavy with bright green algae. Her wine, held aloft in painted nails, was a vivid splash of red against it.

"You think she did it, don't you?" I whispered.

Veronica let out a long shudder. "I'm almost certain she did."

"What's changed?"

"Nothing. I've just had time to think. Everything comes together so neatly against her."

"It's almost," I said, "as if I'm the only one left in the world who doesn't think she did it."

"Wait. I thought you said everyone suspected Brian now?"

"Most everyone does, yeah. But anyone who really knows Maya thinks she did it. And that's what worries me the most. That inevitably the police will realize what's right in front of them and turn their focus back toward her."

"I guess — I don't know if I should be telling you this — but I had a visitor yesterday who made me face my own doubts. A lovely sort of man-woman."

Veronica's way of saying it made me smile despite myself. Made Blake into some ancient mythological creature. But the smile vanished as I realized the significance of what she was saying. "Blake came here? What for?"

"Oh, you've met her? She wanted to find Maya. Apparently Maya owes her money. Drug money."

"God. What did you say?"

"Nothing. Why should I know about anything like that? I told her Maya was missing. She didn't believe me at all. Said she'd be back, next time with a friend. I said I'd call the police if she ever returned. She laughed. I guess she realized my calling the police to my home was pretty unlikely, what with me hiding Maya away somewhere."

"Did she say how much money she thought it was? Or why Maya would have it?"

"She thought Maya offed Jefferson. And that she'd done it to keep his money. He had a lot of cash, apparently, and it's all unaccounted for."

"And you think Maya has it?"

"I don't see how, since you brought her here and she wasn't hiding any money on her. But I guess she could have given it to someone else to hold, or hidden it away some-where. I don't know, frankly. I simply don't know."

My phone vibrated in my pocket. I pulled it out, dread icing my throat. blocked number. I wanted nothing more than to send the call to voice mail. But if I did, I might not hear from Maya again for days. And I needed her close to me. I needed to know precisely what she was up to.

"Hello?" I said. But it wasn't Maya. It was an old man's voice. "Hello? Is this Abigail Goodwin?"

"Yes. Who's this?" I asked, crossing to the other side of the living room and pressing a finger to my free ear.

"My name's Ernest Novotny. I own the gas station across from the school? You see me every day or so?"

"Okay. Yeah, Ernie. Wouldn't have ever expected you to call me."

"I was wondering if you'd have time to come by and talk. This afternoon, if possible."

"Sure, I guess. What's this about?"

"I'd rather not say over the phone. I'm here until six. Can you get here before then?"

"Yeah. I'll swing by right away."

"Good. That would be best. Thanks."

I closed my phone.

"Let me guess," Veronica said. "That wasn't Maya."

27.

Ernie was behind the counter, working his way through a line of customers holding sweating gallons of milk or twelve-packs of beer. I slotted myself in at the end of the line. When he saw me, he called his coworker away from restocking ice and had him man the counter. I followed Ernie into his office. I'd never seen anyone walk behind that warped mirrored glass. It felt like I was breaking some secret law.

The tiny room contained scattered papers, a bag of spilled trail mix, a time clock, a television screen, and one chair. "So . . . erm, I'm glad you could come, Abby. Yah, I know you must be real occupied these days. And I'm real sorry Maya's missing. You know she was one of my best customers. Though she probably stole more than she bought!"

He chortled. I thanked him for his concern.

"I got your number from your club card application form. Thank god we keep the numbers for all y'all. A little of abuse of power, there, 'suppose." He smiled, so I assumed there was a joke somewhere in what he'd said. He flicked on the television screen. It showed a security image of the gas pumps outside, the image paused and quivering at the edges. "That boy, Brian? He was in here a couple of days ago, and I saw he was looking real sad and so I asked, 'What's wrong?' Right off, he started telling me about his brother being killed. Whoa. I hadn't known nothing 'bout it — you wouldn't believe what I don't know. Story of my life, right? Anyway, that poor kid. So the next night shift, I had a long stretch with no one needing any gas, I guess, and I figured I'd take a look at my security footage from the night Jefferson died, to jog my memory, right? Maybe someone'd been by my store, maybe even a killer! So anyways, stop rambling, Ernie, right? Sorry, anyways, I'm playing it through until I get to this." He pointed to the screen. I looked at the date and time. Three-seventeen A.M. on Saturday morning, a few hours after Jefferson died.

He started it playing.

Her face was turned away, but a girl of just Maya's size — limp hair gleaming in the low-res black-and-white footage, wearing her favorite oversize hoodie with roses and skulls sewn on the back, the one she'd decorated herself and wore all the time — was at the coin-op vacuum at the far side of the gas pumps. You couldn't really see what she was doing, but floor mats were on the ground, and you could occasionally see her arm reach into the trash can. Then she got in the driver's seat, looked around quickly, and drove off.

In Jefferson's car.

The car I'd come across with Cheyenne that very day, spotting Maya's sweatshirt in the backseat.

Ernie and I sat there in silence.

"I'm glad you showed me this," I finally said.

"So what do we do now?" Ernie said.

"Have you called the police?" I asked. "Has anyone else seen this?"

"No," he said.

"Could I ask you. " I said, trying to keep my breathing under control, "not to turn this in to them?"

He picked through the trail mix until he found a chocolate piece and popped it into his mouth. Finally, he spoke. "I'd be happy to have nothing to do with the police till the end of my days. They've been trying to shut me down since I bought this stupid place. Bullies. And I have no sympathy for that boy who died. He was half the reason I kept getting in trouble, him and his pretty boy friends causing hell in here, dealing in the parking lot where I couldn't see, then trying to charm their way out. It was . . . condescending, was what it was. If your Maya had something to do with his death, I'm not going to be the one to turn her in. I intend to destroy the recording, is what I intend to do, if you'll permit me being frank about it."

"So that's the whole reason you called me? To tell me that I don't have to worry?"

"I saw you and that friend of yours come by earlier today, looking nervous. I know y'all've been searching out everything you can about your sister. You wouldn't want this recording getting out, I'm sure, but you should know if Maya's been leaving a trail all over the county, right? You'll need to be finding out where else she might have gotten to that night. Who else might have her captured on video. Stuff like that."

"Well," I started, plotting my words carefully, "the truth is, I'm finding it hard to get her to even acknowledge that she did anything wrong at all that night. If you'd give me the recording, I could let her know what's on it. Maybe even show it to her, somehow. It might get her to come to terms with reality a little. In any case, I'd feel better having it in my hands." My reasoning sounded pretty bogus, even by Ernie standards; all I knew was that I wanted to be the one in control of the recording.

"I can erase it. That's easy enough."

"But the police could come in and see that you have an erased section. That wouldn't look good. And even erased files leave traces. Is it on a disk? You could just give it to me. I'd feel much better that way. I'm her sister. I know what's best for Maya."

He scrutinized me for a moment, then pressed a button. A disc emerged from the machine. "If you think it's best, sure. What do I know? Here you go."

I slid it between two pages of my planner, thanked him, and sped toward the door. "Hey, Abby," Ernie called as I left, "stay good, okay?"

I didn't answer, just gave him a quick wave because my phone was ringing again. I flipped it open as soon as I was outside.

This time it was Maya.

"Abby?"

"Is it really you?" I gushed into the phone, my voice quaking crazily. "Thank god. I've been thinking about you all the time. I'm so glad you've finally called. I know you're scared about what's happening, and I know I said everyone thinks it's Brian that did it, not you, but it's not so clear anymore; apparently he was home playing video games, so you should stay put and if you really feel like coming home, make it clear that you were already suspicious of him, oh, I'm just so glad you called —"

"Shut up for a second," she said. "What's got you so worked up?"

"What's got me worked up? What do you mean, what's got me worked up? Have you been listening to me? You're on the run from a murder investigation — is that enough for you?"

"Seriously, you have to calm down. You sound crazy."

"I'm spinning hard right now, I guess. Where are you?"

"I'm really not supposed to say," Maya said. "Veronica made me promise."

"Are you safe?"

"Yeah, unless you count boredom. In that case I'm doomed."

"Are you at someone's house?"

"Yeah. It's a house. The police looking for me?"

"Uh-huh. Like, nonstop."

"I don't think I can face them. For a while I thought I wouldn't ever need to. But I don't know, Abby, I guess I realized I can't live on the run forever. What would I do with myself? I'd have to just move somewhere and wipe my identity. I have no idea how that works. And I can't just keep on leeching off Veronica, either."

"It sounds miserable."

"Yeah. So I'm not going to do it anymore."

"It's not a slam-dunk case against Brian anymore. But if you're insisting on coming back, I think we should get our parents involved. Dad won't let anything happen to you. He'll know who to talk to, how to position things, and all that."

She took a deep breath before answering.

28.

Maya crash-landed back into our lives late that night, hurtling onto the driveway from the back of Veronica's convertible. Veronica left her on the curb and sped off before my parents could see her. Maya stood in the street for a few minutes, swaying in the dark and staring at her old home. I knew because I was watching from my window.

I wondered if she was debating whether or not to come inside. She raised her hands up to the rail of the parked boat, as if she were stretching. Her face was hidden; the only thing that betrayed her uncertainty was that she kept giving her duffel bag little kicks. It rolled with a nylon whisking sound, then reluctantly eased back to its shape, like an old abused pet. She heaved it to her shoulder and then backed down the driveway, as though she might flee and hitchhike away somewhere. But she didn't. She went to the front door. I heard the doorbell ring, heard my parents grunt and stir. I waited to hear their gasps and exclamations.

I heard the front door open and close. But beyond that sound, the house stayed silent. I had hoped someone would come fetch me from upstairs, that Dad would show up at my door and say, "Abby, thank you! Your sister is *home*." But my only company remained the television flickering at the foot of my bed. *Stop being a child. Don't sit here waiting to be found. Your little sister is downstairs. She needs you. Go find her.*

I still couldn't hear a noise as I crept downstairs, except for Cody's sighing and panting. For a flash I imagined that Maya had killed our parents, gassed or garroted them. It would have been effortless, to execute them in stillness and then come for me.

They were all in the kitchen, Maya slumped against a door and my parents seated at the table. Dad had taken up smoking again, apparently; he leaned back in his chair until it connected with the wall, pressed his head against the wallpaper, resting on the lush bed of his black curls. He watched Maya like she was a performing animal that might start juggling at any moment. Mom rested her head on her hands, like a student lost in a lecture.

If they'd been hooting and hugging, or even fighting and yelling, I could have understood and followed their lead. But I couldn't figure out my role in this silence. I stood at the doorway. "Hey, Maya, you're back," I said.

As we'd agreed, she didn't betray any sign of having made contact with me. She just nodded in my direction.

I sort of got why our parents were paralyzed: Their daughter had returned, but they didn't really know her any-more; she'd spun far away enough by now that she was no longer in orbit. If they acknowledged she was theirs again, they could lose her again. And they *would* lose her — for all they knew, she was a killer destined for jail. But I couldn't stand to see Maya alone in their presence, slumped against the door. I knew what she'd endured to get herself here, what emotional contortions she'd put herself through to face what she'd most feared. She'd never done that before, turned and faced the beast instead of dodging and bolting. I crossed through the silence and, ignoring our parents' stares at my back, hugged my sister.

Her breath was sweet against my neck. She didn't get up, so I hunched and curled with her. I let myself fall to the floor, and together we pivoted and faced our parents.

Dad's voice was low, unusually low. "You have no idea, Maya, you have no idea of what you've put us through —"

"Dad, this is hardly the time," I said. "Can't you give her five minutes before you start — "

"I will not!" he bellowed, standing. "I won't give her five *seconds* of peace after everything she's done. Look at your mother. Do you think she's slept more than a few hours any night in the last week? No one would have claimed that Maya ever behaved herself well, but this is beyond it all. The shock, the dishonesty of it all . . ."

"Don't you want to know if I did it?" Maya asked.

"No!" Dad said. "I don't want you to say the words."

"Don't say anything, darling," Mom said hollowly. "We'll always love you, no matter what you've done."

Maya started shaking. Not from rage, but from something sadder and more primal. That unnamed emotion we all feel the split second before rage.

216

"It wasn't Maya," I said angrily. "They think Brian did it now."

"What do you know about the inner workings of the police department?" Dad asked.

"So you think your daughter's a killer?" I challenged. "Is that it?"

Mom and Dad exchanged a look. He slammed out of his chair and headed to the den.

"Where are you going?" I yelled. No answer.

Once he'd gone, my mom came to life. She pulled an assortment of herbal teas down from the cupboard. "How about a nice pomegranate chamomile?"

We all hated pomegranate chamomile. It stained our mouths red and made us look like five-year-olds who had gotten into the Kool-Aid. But Maya and I accepted, and we all sat around the table. Mom asked her, quietly, where she'd been staying. Maya refused to say. She didn't really say anything to either of us, but just smiled each time we tried to get her to talk. A tiny smile, but a real one.

Dad didn't return to the kitchen. I imagined him smoking in the club chair in the den, eavesdropping on our conversation, unable to face his shapeshifting daughter.

I realized how very wrong I was, though, when I heard the front door unlock. There wasn't a key sound, just the slide of the deadbolt; it had been unlocked from the inside.

Mom, Maya, and I all paused, Maya in mid-sip. From the driveway came the sound of an engine cutting off. "Go," Mom whispered urgently to Maya. "Out the back. Go!"

There I was, trying to empathize with Dad's sense of betrayal, when the proof of *his* betrayal was literally at the door. Maya and I sat still for a horrible second, motionless in blinding incomprehension, then simultaneously shoved back from the table. Maya snatched her duffel and we split for the back door, through the den. But we pulled up short; Dad had dragged the heavy sectional to block the back door. We probably could have moved it, but there wasn't time to even try. I could hear the clomp of boots coming through the front door.

Police officers. And us with nowhere to go.

I stood protectively over Maya and felt a flood of warmth surge against my cold panic as she gave under my embrace and folded into me. "Let them try to take you," I whispered to her. "Just let them try. No need to run. I won't let them hurt you."

I heard my mother scream in protest, heard Dad yell at her to stay out of the way. Heard Jamison's low voice, then saw Alcaraz at the entrance to the den. He took in the sight of us, cowering on a club chair, my body around Maya's, and slowly shook his head.

29.

We sat around the dining room table: our parents along one edge, Maya and I along the next, and then the two detectives. We were three teams, each with its own goals, each with its own weapons.

"Everyone at school says it was Brian Andrews," I was saying.

"Abby, please be quiet," Dad said. He'd been presiding over us, steering his daughters like a committee. "Let Detective Alcaraz speak."

"Thank you," Alcaraz said. His hair was ungelled; I wondered if he'd been pulled out of bed. "Let's start at the most basic level. Maya, could you tell me where you were the night that Jefferson Andrews died?"

She'd shrieked at first, cowered at the back door of the den, refused to talk to the police. But once a few minutes had gone by and they still hadn't arrested her, she'd calmed down some. It seemed they wanted to talk to her, not haul her in. It still didn't look good, but it was better than we'd first assumed. "I was there early on," Maya said. "I saw Jefferson at the Bend. We had a fight. But that was it. I spent the night with a friend down at Medusa's Den. The tattoo place on Langdell."

"Did you strike Mr. Andrews?"

Maya let out a guttering breath. "Yes. But lightly!"

"Lightly?" Jamison prompted, smiling thinly.

"Not hard enough to kill anyone," Maya said stubbornly. "Look at me. I couldn't kill anything."

"If you surprise someone, and you're angry, it's very possible. I've seen women smaller than you take down boys bigger than Jefferson."

"*Please,*" Mom said, worrying a napkin between her fingers.

"And you're claiming you only hit him once?" he continued.

"Definitely."

I went rigid, then forced myself to relax. Hadn't Brian said the police concluded that Jefferson had been struck multiple times? I tried to remember his body, what it would look like to an examiner. It looked like there had only been that one wound on his head, but it had certainly been deep.

"Were you under the influence of any mind-altering substances at the time?"

"Drugs? No. I'd had some pot, that was all." Spoken like a true hard drug user — she tossed marijuana around like it was a multivitamin.

"And did you remove Jefferson's car from the Bend?"

"No," Maya said.

"Maya . . ." I said warningly.

"It's clearer to me now, Abby," she protested. "I was

confused then, but I'm sure I didn't. You don't just forget something like that, no matter what state you're in."

Alcaraz looked meaningfully between Maya and me and opened his mouth to speak. I beat him to it. "Have you guys located Jefferson's car?" I asked.

"Yes," Alcaraz said. I caught the warning look Jamison shot at him, glancing up quickly from his furious scribbling of notes.

"So you didn't," Alcaraz said, "provide the illegal substances that we detected in Jefferson Andrews's bloodstream the night he died?"

"What?" Maya said, confused.

"Forensics have come back," he said, "showing large amounts of heroin in his system. Anything you can clue us in about?"

Dad scratched his ear. Anyone who didn't know him well wouldn't have thought anything of it. But I could sense his mind firing, knew he was thinking about the drugs he'd found in Maya's room.

"I don't know what you're talking about," Maya said, staring around the table. "Does anyone here know what this is about?"

No one answered.

"Anyone want to come to my defense here? Abby," Maya said, "I thought you told me everyone was absolutely positive that Brian did it."

I shook my head. "I don't know anymore."

"You're not taking her in tonight?" Dad asked sullenly. It wasn't really a question, and we all knew it. He wasn't going to let his daughter be hauled away. In return for our goodwill, he expected them to allow us to keep Maya.

"No," Alcaraz said with an unconvincing smile. "Not enough evidence. At this point."

"Because she didn't *do* it," I said.

The officers excused themselves and left. Maya immediately went into the kitchen, snatched her duffel, and headed for her basement room. Dad, however, blocked the way. "Don't you dare," Maya seethed, "even *try* to talk to me."

"Listen to me good," Dad said, his voice starting quiet and gradually increasing to a roar. "You're not calling any shots around here anymore, do you hear me? You've run roughshod over your mother and me for years, and now you're going to *listen*. You've vanished for a *week*, and seem to think you can come back and act like queen of the manor. Well, I won't stand for it. I just won't. And you can sleep in your normal room, not the basement. No more of this sick subterranean life."

"You're my *father*," Maya wailed. "And you called the *police* on me."

"I'll have you know that the only reason you're home right now and not in jail," Dad said, "is because we called them as soon as you arrived. Establishing our good faith is everything in a case like this. We are living in complete honesty from here on out, do you understand?" He turned to include me as well.

I pretended to be heading up to my bedroom. "Don't bring *me* into this," I sulked, speaking over my shoulder. "You two have enough to tackle without starting in on me."

"Do neither of you see how important this is?" Dad yelled. "Don't you see how much is on the line?"

"Oh yeah, *Dad*," Maya said, "I see exactly how much is on the line. Your reputation. Big shot local lawyer. Which is why you're taking the police's side over your own daughter's. Because you threw me to the wolves a long time ago, didn't you? Who cares about that little bitch Maya? Good riddance, right?"

He slapped her. Not hard, but he caught her off balance so she careened into the wall. He clenched her chin in his hand before she could fall. "Don't dare say that. I would do anything to keep you safe, do you understand that? Anything."

She nodded, as much as she could in his meaty grip. The thing was, we believed him. He was the equilibrium in our lives. As cold and steady as justice. When we wronged, we could look for no compassion. When someone wronged us, he would become revenge itself.

I guess I was trying to follow in his footsteps.

SATURDAY, MAY 18

30.

Maybe Maya couldn't stand the idea of being by herself after having lived alone for so many days. Maybe she wanted to bond and was finally planning on letting me inside. Maybe that crazy basement room of hers was too depressing. Whatever the reason, she showed up in my doorway as I was preparing for bed. I pulled back the comforter and she slid in.

I got up to pee during the night, and when I came back, I could see Maya's eyes gleaming. I wondered if she'd slept at all — she'd been tossing all night. "Where did Veronica have you stay?" I asked once it was obvious neither of us would be falling asleep anytime soon.

"One of the art professors at the junior college is on sabbatical," she whispered. "Veronica had a key to water his plants, so she let me stay there. It wasn't too bad. There was premium cable. Some hilarious gay porn hidden under the bed."

We fell into a comfortable late-night silence. "Blake's looking for you," I said after a while.

"You met Blake? Jeez, what didn't you do to try to help me?"

Maya was proud of me, for once, and I wasn't about to

start unloading my frustrations and jinx it. "I was worried about you. Anyway, Blake claims you have some money that Jefferson owed her. Fifteen thousand dollars."

"Wow."

"Do you?"

"No, of course not. I'd be totally gone if I did. Do you think Jefferson would trust me with any of his money? He paid me in drugs."

"Are you still . . . getting high?"

"No way. I treated my undercover time as a sort of accidental detox program."

"Good idea."

"Don't start thinking of me as some kind of saint. It's not like I had much of an option."

"I guess the only reason I bring up Blake is to make sure you don't go finding her. It wouldn't be pretty. She's mad."

"I'm not going to go finding anyone. If I have my way, I'll be hanging out at home for a good long time."

"No going back to school, huh?"

"Bah. Why start now? Maybe I'll start studying for my GED again. Except without any hot tutors this time." She ran a hand through her hair. She hadn't showered yet, and didn't seem to have cleaned up for quite a few days. "You know," she said, "I think Blake could have done it. Killed Jefferson."

"I've thought of that," I said.

"Think about it. Jefferson was skimming off the top of

their deals. She couldn't let that go unpunished. She had plenty of excuse to be royally pissed."

"And did you see those arms?" I said. "Girl is buff. But still, while we're on the topic, what do you think of Brian being guilty?"

"I don't know. It's hard to believe. He's so . . . quiet. Sweet. But then again, that's what they always say about killers on the news."

"What about Rose?"

Maya snorted. "Totally capable. But why would she kill Jefferson? She probably would have killed *me* first. Or done some gory double homicide type thing."

"Well, you weren't there. Who knows what actually went down?"

"Who else are you thinking?"

I sighed. I guessed I could've offered Cheyenne, too, but that still didn't seem likely to me, despite the blackmail Jefferson had on her with the plagiarized essays and her new position as recipient of the Florida's Scholars money. "Nobody."

"Let's not talk about it anymore," Maya said sleepily. "I don't want to keep letting my life revolve around Jefferson. He can't have even more power over me dead than he did alive. That just can't happen."

"Okay," I said, snuggling close to her. "Then we won't let him."

But of course he did. We knew our lives would revolve around him for a long time, possibly forever. It was thanks to him that we hardly slept that night. It was thanks to him that, somewhere over the course of her dreams, Maya screamed.

The sound woke me up, and I curled around her while I dozed. She quickly fell back asleep, but I never did. I lay there, not daring to move in case I woke her. Poor wild creature, scared and trusting. I could only lie there for so long, though, before my thoughts started skidding and I began to bug out. There was no way I'd be doing any sleeping. I untangled myself from her, placing a pillow against her so she would still think I was there, then headed down the hallway.

The door to our parents' room was slightly ajar, as was their habit. I peeked in as I went down the hall to the bathroom. I could see Mom on the far side of the bed, her body curved toward the wall, head shrouded by the pillow she kept draped over it to drown out Dad's snores. I ducked my head inside the door to see whether Dad was there next to her.

He wasn't.

31.

Maya," I said, shaking her awake. "Maya!"

"What?" she groaned, disoriented. "Let me sleep!"

"It's Dad," I whispered. "He's out front, waiting for some-one. I think he called the police."

She sat up, swiped at her face. "What?"

"Get your shoes on, now!" I was already tossing things around the room. Maya grabbed a pair of flip-flops. She was wearing only that, a T-shirt over bra and panties and a pair of flip-flops, as she dashed with me down the back stairs.

I wished I had a few more seconds to think. My mom had made my dad replace the sectional sofa the night before, so we could get out the back door . . . but what then?

"Where do we go?" I asked, my voice panicky.

"We take your car," Maya said.

"No," I said sharply. "My car's in front, where Dad is. We can't risk him stopping us."

It was all decided by a crash. Dad had knocked over a lamp in the hallway. Maya glanced back and screamed. I was vaguely aware of a large shape bearing down on us. I snatched Maya's arm and pulled us through the back door.

We skirted the pool and made for the fence. I put one

foot against the gray slats and hoisted Maya over. Once she had crashed to the other side I followed. I glanced back while I went over the top and saw Dad surging across the grass.

We landed in a thicket of tall reeds, a creek running among them. We could follow it in either direction, and if we made it a few dozen feet before my dad got there and were careful not to rustle the plants, we had a chance of his not knowing which way we went. Maya broke right, so I followed her.

We crashed through the creek. I could think of nothing beyond raising a foot out of the water when it was too deep, or bending back a branch when it was in the way. All I could hear was the gloop of heels pulling through muck; all I could see were gray dawn sky and the reeds and Maya's chopped hair and the tattoo above her waistband, the dark flowery void that had once read *Jefferson*.

Finally, we slowed and paused, listening for sounds of my dad. There weren't any. We'd stumbled upon the perfect escape route — Dad could have gotten in his car and followed us if we'd gone out the front; by breaking for the creek we used our only advantage, our small size. As she cleared a fallen log I saw Maya's bare feet and realized she'd lost her flip-flops. She was bleeding from small scratches along her neck and around her shoulders. I wondered at my own wounds — I couldn't feel any pain, but that was surely thanks to adrenaline.

"I guess we keep going along the creek?" Maya said. It

was really our only option — the vegetation at the edges had thickened, so there was no shore to exit onto.

It was only when we began to move forward again at our slower pace that I realized it — we were heading for the Bend.

Pulse thumping, I tried to think of a way to avoid it. But taking the creek in the other direction would mean going back by my house and getting caught.

It might have taken me miles to run there that horrible morning, but by the direct route of the creek we would be there within minutes. My mind spun, my movements became jerky. But I didn't say anything to Maya — what good would that do?

And then we'd arrived. Yellow police tape dragged in the current. The gravel at the edge was mussed where Jefferson had tried to pull himself onto land. Flipper marks streaked the mud at the shore, where the police's diving teams must have launched to search for evidence.

This was where Jefferson's last hot breaths had been lost in dirt and sludge. Where he had wondered, dazzled and gasping, at the sudden horror of his own death.

"What?" Maya said. I must have stopped moving without realizing it. She was already past the scene, almost around the corner. "What's wrong?"

Of course she didn't sense anything was wrong. She hadn't been the one to find his body. She didn't know this was the exact spot where Jefferson had finally given up and died.

"This is where I found him," I said.

"Oh," Maya said. It was a warm morning, but she was shivering. "Oh, Jesus."

She finally noticed the police tape trailing in the current, the upturned soil at the water's edge. I watched her face collapse in front of me, her large eyes close and only slowly re-open. Then she shook off the moment. "Let's keep going, okay?" she said.

She was right. I followed her determinedly, tried to stop imagining disintegrated bits of Jefferson mingled in the water, molecules of his blood in the eddies around my feet.

The ravine finally sloped and rejoined civilization. We scrambled up a greenish cement drainage ditch and came out at the empty end of a Home Depot parking lot. "I can't go out there," Maya said, sensibly. "I'm almost naked."

I wasn't much better — soaked pajama bottoms with a layer of algae and river grass caking the hem, mud-splattered T-shirt — but she certainly looked much worse. At least I had pants on, after all. Besides, I didn't think she could pull off what I'd have to do. "Okay," I said, "you wait behind the tree line. I'll go see if someone in there will let me use their cell phone."

As I crossed to the store entrance, I couldn't imagine going through with it, being that crazy girl in the crazy rags crazily asking to use someone's cell phone. But as soon as I started walking, I *was* that girl. I decided to try the customer service desk first. It seemed more proper, somehow.

The manager on duty was burly and old, with a rim of

bright silver hair circling a bald perfect circle. He had started smiling at me long before I asked if I could use his phone. I pulled my wet shirt away from my boobs.

"Some days don't go your way, do they?" he said.

"I'd like to make a call."

"Want to walk me through what you've been up to? You been, what, off playing in the creek with some of your friends? You lose your teammates, sweetheart?"

"Hand. Me. The. Phone."

He stammered as I changed in his eyes from sex novelty to potential killer. He swiveled the phone to me, handed me the receiver. "Dial nine first. And take your time," he encouraged, retreating to the opposite side of the customer service desk and immersing himself in a laminated flyer.

I stared at the keypad. Oh god. Hadn't thought about this part. My initial impulse was to call Cheyenne, but that was the first place my parents would look. Veronica's was the second. I had to take Maya to someone they wouldn't think of. Someone with experience in breaking the law. Even if it was a big risk.

I dialed, and Keith answered.

32.

Maya and I looked like hungover mermaids, but Blake and Keith didn't even mention it. They just ushered us into the backseat and sped off toward their apartment. The only sign they made that even acknowledged our weird state was when Blake ran a finger down a muddy streak on Maya's thigh and suggested we take showers as soon as we arrived. I let Maya go first — she'd been shivering on the drive over, and I wanted to see her cleaned up and in warm clothes as soon as possible.

Keith, Blake, and I sat on the couch. They'd put a towel down under me so I wouldn't ruin the upholstery. It was instantly wet.

"So," Blake said, "you planning on telling us what happened?"

I told her that I'd called Maya back at the urging of my parents, only to be betrayed by our father. That we couldn't go back. That Maya was — and I didn't realize it until I said it, not fully — a fugitive from justice, and that I was aiding her. "Abetting," I said, impressed despite myself by the formal term, by my newfound familiarity with the daily danger of Keith and Blake's lives.

Once it became clear they weren't going to kill us, I

decided Keith and Blake were actually a great choice to turn to. Who was less likely to turn in a couple of criminal young ladies, after all, than drug dealers? Christ, what a foursome we made.

They only spoke to me, not to each other, but nevertheless they were holding their own private conversation. Keith transmitted his thoughts to Blake through the long fingertips grazing her shoulder, and Blake responded by quivering her lip or darning her eyebrows. I watched something deflate inside Blake; now that she'd seen how pathetic we looked, she was satisfied that Maya and I weren't crafty schemers cheating her out of her money. "You and Maya can stay as long as you need," she said finally, smack in the middle of one of my rambling sentences.

"Thank you! Thank you so much," I said.

"It's Saturday morning — back to bed, waffles at noon?" Keith proposed to Blake, smirking. I glanced at the clock — 8:50. Not even nine in the morning, and what a full day it had already been.

Maya came out of the bathroom right as Blake and Keith had finished stripping and arranging themselves in bed. She rummaged through a drawer, found a clean pair of Keith's underwear to put on, and handed me her towel. I thanked her and took it into the bathroom.

The shower curtain rail was white and slimy, the tiles grouted in stripes of green-black bacteria, but how good that shower felt! At first it was just the joy of seeing mud run off my legs and stopper the drain until it gurgled away, my feet pink and healthy against the vanishing black, and then it was the heat, that cleansing heat. But beyond the amazing physical sensations, it was having time by myself to think, time in which no one was going to start bringing me fresh dramas. In the shower I didn't have to plan my life. How good it felt to let go, even if for just fifteen minutes.

When I came out, Maya was already snoozing in the bed with Blake and Keith. I opened the drawer she'd sifted through and picked out clean(ish) briefs, a pair of sweat-pants, and a soft wrinkled dress shirt. I'd go braless, I guessed. A first for Abby Goodwin.

I stood in the middle of the room, unsure of what to do with myself. Snoring filled the apartment.

Before I'd turned to Blake and Keith, I'd been an agent off the map — I might not have been sure of what to do at each turn, but I never had to worry about being personally impli-cated in the growing investigation. But now I'd officially done wrong in the eyes of my parents and the police. I couldn't walk outside openly anymore without risking dis-approval or even arrest. I was, in short, experiencing what it meant to be Maya.

Maybe it's a mark of the guilty that they seek out the approval of the innocent. All I knew — no, it wasn't "know-ing," it was an emotion, as intense and as undeniable as sorrow — was that I didn't want to spend the next episode of this tortured story in this hideout with Maya, Blake, and Keith. I wanted to be with my parents, mainly, but since that wasn't an option, I wanted to be with someone the world hadn't condemned. Someone clean.

Making sure no one was awake, I took Keith's phone into the bathroom and called Cheyenne. She picked up immediately, and I could sense the upset in her voice. As I'd guessed, Dad had already called her to see where I was. She promised to lie to him if he called again. She also promised to meet me downstairs within half an hour. I crept downstairs.

I expected to encounter some rough types while I waited, but apparently nine-thirty A.M. is an off-hour for druggies. Cheyenne pulled up in her old green jalopy, rolled down the window, and yelled out for me to hop in. I loved how she said it so casually, like we were in a seventies TV show and I should jump through the door window, like we were in a carefree world and I hadn't called her from a drug den to pick me up because I was a fugitive from the police. (A fugitive from my dad? I didn't really have my dad and the police distinct in my head anymore. They'd pretty much melded.)

"Where're we going?" she asked.

"Anywhere but here," I hooted, keeping up our seventies TV show thing.

"All right, ma'am."

We hit the road. I told her as much as I could. The structure of my world had twisted so quickly recently that nothing I said was in the right order, nothing was a lie and nothing was the truth. I could see her working to keep everything straight. But I could always rely on the sorting power of her brain; she figured it all out silently and didn't need to ask any questions.

"What's going on in *your* life?" I asked.

"Nothing." She laughed. "Compared to you, absolutely nothing."

"Talk to me about nothing," I sighed. "That sounds great."

"Okay," Cheyenne said, tapping the wheel. "Why do you think neither of us have had any serious boyfriends?"

"Oh! Heavier than I was expecting, but okay. I guess because all the guys at our school are lame."

I knew how unlikely that sounded, though. Really? Every single guy at Xavier High? Cheyenne seemed to see through my exaggeration: She got the constipated look she reserved for boys and dissection labs. "But even guys outside of school, you know? It's not like our town's empty. I feel so behind the curve. Everyone else has been having sex since forever, but us . . . nah. I understand me, I know I'm not that pretty, but you —"

"Um, shut up. You're totally pretty."

"I'm serious, Abby. What is it? You've had a couple of guys, but you got bored with each one after, what, a month? Three weeks?"

"I don't know. When I fall, I fall hard. But it doesn't happen that much."

"How can you be so sure it will, when it never has before?"

I pressed my head against the window and stared at the scenery. For two people without a destination, I realized, we were driving pretty fast. "Where are we going?" I said casually.

"Hmm?" Cheyenne said, not looking up from the road. "You'll see."

"No. Absolutely not. No surprises," I said. "Stop the car."

But she didn't slow down. She made a screeching turn, zoomed up a ramp, and suddenly we were on the interstate.

"Cheyenne," I said, "where are we going?"

No response.

I swallowed against my rising panic. "Cheyenne, where were you the night Jefferson died?"

"I told you. I was at the mall, closing up."

"At one in the morning?"

"We were doing inventory."

"I can't believe that you'd be allowed to be there that late."

"It's funny that you bring that up right now," she said. "Because you're right — I lied about where I was."

"Why is that funny?"

"You'll find out. Isn't it crazy how everything comes together at once?"

"No!" I said hotly. "I will not 'find out.' You'll tell me right now."

"Haven't you realized where we're going yet?"

"No," I said bitterly. I was so not in the right mood for a stupid riddle game. And I was scared.

"Veronica's. We're going to Veronica's."

"Why?"

She shook her head. I couldn't exactly throw myself out of a moving car, and I didn't want to say anything that would cause me to lose my best ally, so I sat quietly and seethed. I would have been terrified if my anger hadn't been so strong.

Veronica was home, of course. And expecting us — incense was burning in the window. She opened the door as we were approaching.

"Hello, my cherubs," she said.

"Hey, Veronica," Cheyenne said.

I blinked, looking from one to the other. "You two sure are chummy, aren't you?" I said.

"Come on, Abby, let's go," Cheyenne said, ushering me inside.

Veronica was up to her usual, offering us mimosas, which we accepted and then proceeded not to drink. She wanted to know the latest updates, and listened gravely. It didn't quite seem like news to her; she nodded before I'd finished each sentence. "Cheyenne," I concluded, "is just about to tell me what she was doing the night Jefferson died."

Veronica looked at her meaningfully. "Really? You are?"

At that moment I could feel my pulse without moving a finger; the edges of my vision surged with each pound of my heart. "Cheyenne," I asked, "what are you about to tell me?"

She reached under the neck of her shirt and pulled out a

key on a chain, the key I'd noticed in the car the week before. "Shall I?" she asked Veronica.

"There's no way to turn back now," Veronica said, a little ticked. "Now that the cat's out. You could have told her you were here with me and left it at that, couldn't you? But there's no turning back now. Go ahead."

Cheyenne stepped toward the back of the house. I knew where she was headed: the locked room.

33.

What could Veronica and Cheyenne possibly have hidden behind that door? My imagination didn't go anywhere; I was too overwhelmed. I stood and watched.

"You can't tell Maya what you're about to see," Cheyenne said as she pulled out the key I'd seen on the chain around her neck. I didn't say anything. No way was I making any promises.

Veronica hovered near the kitchen as Cheyenne fitted her key into the heavy lock. She pushed the door open.

I'd braced for something sinister and unholy. But it was, perhaps, the most radiant room you could imagine. The walls had been papered a yellow halfway between butter and yolk; a small window at the end faced a box of paper tulips. Shelves, pink and blue, had been decorated with knickknacks that must have been bought in one swoop from the same cutesy store: rabbits, Buddhas, and clay globes all shone with the same high gloss. On the bed grazed a motley pack of stuffed animals, a tiger curled sleepily around a panda on the pillow. I stepped into the cotton candy of the room and swiveled.

"Isn't it great?" Veronica called from the hallway. "Won't she just love it?"

"It's the most ridiculous thing I've ever seen. And won't *who* just love it?" I whispered to Cheyenne.

"Maya," she whispered back. "Veronica wants her to move in with her. I helped her set up the room after my shift. And there's no better time for Maya to come than now, right?"

"What? Does Maya know about this?"

Cheyenne shook her head. "Veronica wanted to get the room perfect and then surprise her."

I sat down on the bed. It sighed potpourri. "So she wanted to take her from my mom and dad."

"They barely had her, anyway, right? Veronica wanted to see her have a stable place, an actual home to turn to instead of druggies' couches. A parent figure she'd still be open to."

"And you were helping her in this insane plan?" I asked.

Veronica's cats, intrigued by the smells in the new room, came in and started tapping their noses against the carpet. "Look," Cheyenne said, "I was tired of seeing Maya rule you. I didn't want her to keep taking up all of your time, and I wanted to see her have something stable in her life. You might not think I'm that tight with her, but I've grown up alongside Maya, just by knowing you. Don't shoot me down for trying to do what's best for both of you."

"Why didn't Veronica just come to me?"

"Because she knew you wouldn't have helped. And" — she held up a hand against my protest — "*you* know you wouldn't have helped. You'd have been weird about it. You can't deny it."

"Actually," I said, "it's been becoming clearer and clearer that you really *don't* know me. There's no way I would have been weird about it. I'd have been relieved that other people were trying to help. And you needed me on the inside on this — do you think there's any way my parents would have been okay with Maya moving here without me working on them first? I'm the link between her and my parents. Without my blessing, she does nothing." What got me most was Cheyenne's tone. As if (supposedly) knowing my inner thoughts made her superior to me.

"It was all with the best intentions," Cheyenne said. "But what's going on right now is precisely why I never told you. I knew you'd react just like this."

"They're not the best intentions, even if you think they are," I said, pressing the door closed behind us. A cherub mobile tinkled. "Veronica might be really friendly, but she's also the loneliest woman ever. And she's doing all this so that she'll have someone living here with her."

"So what?" Cheyenne said, taking the spot on the bed I'd just left. "So it fills two people's needs at the same time. Three, if you count having responsibility for Maya off your back. What's so wrong with that?"

I couldn't find words to explain why it felt wrong. I guess I thought people should be entirely altruistic or entirely self-ish, not some sloppy mix of the two. I didn't say anything, because I knew, even as I thought them, that my views weren't rational, and I could sense Cheyenne lording her implied victory over me. The same qualities that made me cling to her when I was in trouble made me hate her when she surprised me.

"It's so wrongheaded," I said.

Cheyenne wrinkled her nose. "Wrongheaded? What kind of pretentious word is that?"

That only got me more angry. I'd captured exactly what I wanted to say: that this scheme was both dumb and done for the wrong reasons. "Look at the way you guys have decorated it," I said. "Yellow wallpaper. Stuffed animals. Maya's fifteen. She's got piercings in places you don't want to know. Did you really think she'd like this room?"

The door creaked open. Veronica had been listening in; I'd suspected as much. "I don't think you're giving your sister much credit," she said, tilting into the room and laying fingers on all the trite garbage she'd bought. "Just because Maya expresses her dark side easily doesn't mean that she doesn't have a light core. In fact, it would indicate the opposite — we're all in dynamic opposition, the conscious presentation giving the lie to the soul."

I rolled my eyes in Cheyenne's direction. "No wonder you two get along so well."

"She's right," Cheyenne said. "Maybe Maya's looking for a little something in her life that's earnest and kind. Something she can scoff at on the outside and be grateful for on the inside."

"Fine, whatever," I said. "But she can't hide here — it's too risky. So your lame idea is automatically nixed."

I wanted out of there. I hated what Veronica had

implied — that what everyone seemed to be was a lie, that sweet people were afraid of some core cruelty, that mean people were protecting some fragile inner kindness. And yet her words had jabbed through and had me questioning myself. The kindness behind Veronica's impulse to create Maya a room of her own, however misguided, had moved me deeply. I did much better with harshness; harshness, I knew how to handle.

What was it in me that sought it out, that kept returning to the darkest places? I broke things down, over and over, even as the outside me accepted everyone with generosity and openness. I was a generous cynic, an honest liar.

I bolted from that secret, childish room. "I'm sure Maya would love it," I hissed from the doorway, "if she weren't doomed. But she'll never live here with you, Veronica, because she'll never be anywhere but prison. No matter what any of us do."

34.

So now Cheyenne had an alibi — and a much better one than Brian's or Maya's. This should have made me relieved — my best friend wasn't a killer! — but instead it left me only sad and disoriented.

I left the house without any idea of where to go or how to get there. I'd walked as far as the subdivision entrance when a police cruiser pulled up alongside me.

I watched Detective Alcaraz get out. He had his arms folded, but he released them and held them forward, palms up. Like he had to prove to me that he didn't mean any harm, like I was an armed criminal. "There's no point in trying to escape."

"I'm not going to try to escape," I said sullenly.

"Will you come to your grandmother's house with me and talk, then?"

It was almost reassuring, settling into the front seat of his cruiser, smelling fabric and smoke and cardboard. I numbly drank in his details. He must own at least two different kinds of police shirts; the one before had been too tight, but this one was loose, the collar hanging low on the back of his neck, revealing a fringe of dark back hair. Alcaraz parked in Veronica's driveway and walked me into her living room. I was already so emotional, it had me on the verge of tears that he trusted me not to turn and flee. Maybe he was aware of how futile my running would have been.

"Did you do this? Did you call him?" I hissed at Veronica as I walked inside.

"No," she said, staring at Alcaraz in alarm.

"Really! He just showed up?!" But Veronica looked genuinely confused. If she hadn't called him, who had?

Alcaraz sat down on the couch. "Yes. I just showed up."

"Are you here to arrest me, or something?"

"Why don't you take a seat, Abby?" Veronica said.

I remained standing.

"What would I arrest you for?" Alcaraz asked.

"I helped Maya escape," I said flatly. "But I'm gonna bet you already know that."

"I've got larger concerns than a girl looking out for her sister," Alcaraz said. "What you need to realize, though, is that the best way to *continue* to protect her is to help us find her. Remember those seventy-two hours I mentioned last time we spoke? They're long up. Soon the Feds will swoop in and start beating in doors. After that everyone's options become very limited. Do you understand what I mean? We're in our final moment."

I glanced at Veronica, pale and nodding from a bar stool in the kitchen. "Where's Cheyenne?" I asked. Veronica gestured my attention back toward Alcaraz. I glanced at the closed door to that spare room. My best friend was hiding from me.

"Abby?" Alcaraz asked. "Have you been listening to me?"

"Yes, sir," I said. I had intended for my words to come out politely, but they definitely didn't.

"We need you to turn your sister in," he said severely. "You have to know where she's hiding. I need you to go get her and bring her to me."

"No chance," I said.

"I don't think you understand," he said. "If you don't agree to what I'm asking right now, I'll name you an obstruction to justice and bring you into custody."

"Custody!" Cheyenne said, emerging from the secret room. "You didn't say anything about that. You can't."

I leaped to my feet. "You make this happen, Cheyenne? You call the police here for the good of everyone? Not going exactly as you planned, eh?" I spat.

"Sit down," Alcaraz said, at the same time Veronica said, "Cheyenne's only trying to do what's best for you and Maya."

"I'm tired of 'what's best!'" I shot back. "If what's best had happened, then Jefferson wouldn't be dead. No one would be under questioning for anything. So no one pretend to have any idea what I should be doing right now. And did you know who called in that tip about the body? It was someone in this room. It wasn't me, and it wasn't Veronica."

"Abby, stop," Cheyenne said.

Alcaraz looked at Cheyenne and me shrewdly. "How's this for 'what's best'? Do what I tell you or I throw you both in jail."

"This is why you called him?" I said to Cheyenne. "To get us thrown in jail?"

"You're in way over your head," Cheyenne said softly.

I gestured toward Veronica. "She's seventy. And now she's going to end up spending the last years of her life in jail. So that was a real good thing you did, Cheyenne. Thanks so much for that."

"Look," Alcaraz said, "no one needs to go to jail, if you cooperate fully. Forensics has come back telling us that Jefferson was high when he died. We know your sister had access to drugs, that she was a dealer —"

"*He* was the dealer! She worked under *him*."

"We know that, too," Alcaraz said. "We've also received footage from the gas station across from the high school showing Maya cleaning out Jefferson's car."

"You *what*?" I asked. "Where did you get that?"

"I'm not about to list any police sources to you at this juncture, Ms. Goodwin. Just assume it's anonymous."

I was fighting a multiple-front war, weighing every piece of evidence based on how it affected Maya and Brian and me and Cheyenne all at once. It would be so easy to make a slip; it would be hard enough with just one set of factors and variables, but with many . . . What I needed now was to buy a little time, to hold off Alcaraz until I could set my latest plan into motion.

"What do you need me to do?" I asked softly.

35.

I entered via Medusa's Den, since I'd be able to come in that way without having to buzz up — this would all go much easier, I figured, if Blake and Keith didn't know ahead of time that I was coming. I didn't recognize the front desk attendant, a girl with brown ropy dreads. "Is Keith around?" I asked her, like maybe I came there every day.

"Yeah," she said, thumbing toward the back stairs. "You want me to go get him? You have an appointment?"

"This isn't about a tattoo," I said.

"Piercing?"

"Nope."

"Head on up," she said, returning to doodling in the appointment book.

Each stair made a different creak, sent out a fresh warning.

I didn't knock.

There was only Maya in the room, at the table in her underwear and leaning over a pipe. She didn't hear me coming in; she was intent on the task at hand. "Oh, Maya," I said. "What are you doing?"

She jumped to her feet. Her hands were in her hair. Her skin was fair and shiny, like she hadn't slept in ages. "What are you doing here?" she asked.

"Is anyone else around?" I asked.

"Yeah," she said. "Keep your voice down. They're sleeping." That's when I saw that, yes, two bodies were under the comforter.

"Maya," I said, clutching her close to me and speaking softly and steadily, "you need to get dressed and come down with me. And put that pipe away. I can't *believe* you're using again."

"Why do I have to get dressed?" she said, staring at me uncomprehendingly.

"Just do it," I said. "You're going to have to trust me on this one."

"Um, no," she said. She was really, monstrously high. "And you can't make me trust you. Trust doesn't work like that. Trust is a lot bigger. Like an ocean. You can't just turn on the tap and expect the water level to change."

I rolled my eyes. Maybe it would be easier for her if the police found her high. If they then assumed that she had been drugged when she killed Jefferson. Was that grounds for temporary insanity? At the very least, her vulnerability would make them go easier on her.

"Come on, Maya," I said. "Get dressed and come with me." We only had a few minutes until the police would barge in. It would all go much better if I emerged with her, blinking in the daylight, the girl who went into the drug den and retrieved her little sister. But if she refused to come down, I'd have to become the sudden betrayer, cowering in the corner as the police slammed in, guns drawn and pointed.

"Abby?" Maya said, evidently hitting a pocket of clarity within her highness as she saw my expression. "What's happening to you?"

I was sitting on the floor. I couldn't make myself look anywhere. I mean, my head was moving around, but I couldn't *look anywhere.*

"Abby?" she repeated, louder. "What have you done?!"

"You never should have come back," I mumbled. "You never should have believed me." It felt like I was suffocating.

"Jesus. Jesus!" Maya yelled, dashing around the apartment and rooting clothes out of drawers, whisking through papers and old magazines on the counter, collecting whatever stray money fell out.

Blake sat up in bed. Keith, groggy, was reaching around the floor for a shirt. "What the hell's going on?" he said. "I don't have to work for hours."

"Abby's screwed us over," Blake said, suddenly fully awake and staring at me.

"The cops!" Maya said. "She called the cops on us."

My knees were next to my nose. I guess I'd pulled them there. I nestled my face into the dark space between. All around me I could hear commotion: Keith's curses, Blake's shrill commands, Maya dashing, little footfalls and gasps.

Then, the click of ammunition.

I looked up. Keith was standing by the window blinds with Maya, peering through one of the tiny blank spaces where thread passed through the slats. Blake was standing on one side of the door with a gun, a shiny black thing as long as a forearm, the kind made for wars in foreign countries. "They send you up here as the scout?" she seethed through clenched teeth.

She thought I was less directly involved than I was. I didn't dare to think what she'd do to me if she knew I'd orchestrated all this. "I wanted Maya to come down with me quietly," I explained, "so nothing like this would happen."

"I don't think you have any idea what you're trying to do," Blake said. "First you want to find someone who will get your sister off the hook, and now you're turning her in. I *helped* you, you realize that? Helped you bring the police here. I should end you." She hefted the gun in her hand. Not pointing it at me, but definitely entering it into the conversation.

Even though I was terrified, I didn't feel like my life was in danger. If she was panicked about getting busted, she'd be a fool to add murder to the list. But she was pissed. Crazy pissed.

"What's happening out there?" Blake called to Keith, her voice taking an ever-sharper edge.

"Four of them," he said. "Just in front of the entrance."

"And the other side?"

"I can't see. There's a car parked in the way."

Out of nowhere, a garbled pop song. My phone was ringing in my pocket.

"Your cop friends calling?" Blake barked.

I shook my head timidly.

"Pull it out," she commanded.

I did.

"Look at the screen."

Alcaraz.

"Answer it," Blake said.

It took me a few tries to get the phone open. I kept thinking about the gun, such a heavy weight in her hand. "Hello?" I asked.

"You okay?" Alcaraz asked.

Blake motioned that I should give her the phone. I did, and she started shouting. "You thinking of coming in here," she said, "then you better get ready for a couple of dead teenagers. We know exactly what's happening. We're armed. Tell your boys to back off." She made a motion to Maya, as if to say *Don't worry*, but it was too late for her — Maya was totally bugging out, clawing at Keith's shirt.

I watched Blake listen to Alcaraz's response. Her expression turned from angry to confident, victorious. She hung up the phone and put it away in her own pocket. "They're not going to be coming up anytime soon," she said. "He'd already be up here if they were going to risk barging in."

A thought appeared behind the thrums of my heart: *The police have found out something new; that's why they're backing off.*

"Then can you put the gun away?" Maya wailed. "And don't point it anywhere near my sister." She and Keith watched Blake fearfully.

Instead of putting the gun away, Blake pointed it directly at me. "Actually," she said, "I think it's precisely time that a gun was pointed at your sister."

I put my hands forward, as if to deflect any bullet that might come toward me. I couldn't help but imagine how the physics would work, a steel ball splitting my palm, passing lengthways up my bones, leaving my arm in two drooping red halves as it pierced my chest. "Please," I said, "put the gun away. You know that the police aren't going to come up now, right? So there's really no need for violence." I risked a look in Keith's direction. "Keith, could you make her believe that?"

But he didn't say anything, only stared at me curiously. "What are you onto?" he asked Blake. "What have you figured out?"

She didn't answer. I could feel that bullet passing up my arm again. But this time, it wasn't doing physical damage. She was laying my thoughts open, splitting me in even halves and letting the hidden pearls stream out.

"Why the hell won't she *say* anything?" Maya wailed.

The room was full of the quiet of four raging pulses. Blake didn't lower the gun. Keith looked at me curiously, his arms crossed. Maya trembled at his feet. "Now," I said to Blake, "is not the time for stupid games."

"I'm afraid that now," Blake said, "is the only time that will work. When else will we get you to fess up?" She wiggled the gun. "So start talking."

"What are you *on* about?" Maya cried. I was paralyzed, but Maya got to her feet and took a step toward her. Where did this sudden courage come from? "You're crazy. Put the gun down, okay?"

"You seem to forget that I knew Jefferson Andrews. You couldn't call us friends, but when you're in a profession like ours, you're able to tell your coworkers things you couldn't say to your closest friends."

"Blake," Keith said evenly, "the police are outside. I understand what you're trying to do, but maybe this isn't the time."

"Are you kidding me? How are you two so blind? This is the *only* time. The police aren't going to come in anytime soon, but they're also not going to go away until they have a suspect in custody. And we're going to give them one. Just not the Goodwin girl that they expect."

"Stop," Maya said. "I don't want to hear whatever you're about to say."

"Why not, Maya? Why do you have to be the one to take the fall? Why not your sister here? It's the advantage of being the one who does all the detective work, isn't it, Abby? You get to choose what everyone sees. But I could tell them that Jefferson let me know all about you. I could tell them that Jefferson was scared of you."

I was going to point out that Jefferson had no reason to be scared of me — but it didn't look like Blake was up for an argument. I would have said anything, confessed to anything, to get her to point that gun away from me. I opened my mouth to speak, but Blake continued before I could say anything: "She's got our money, I'm sure of it."

"Slow down, Blake," Keith said. "I doubt Abby has Jefferson's money."

"Tell me you're kidding! I told this little wench all about the fifteen grand he shafted us out of, and she's done nothing but snoop around since then. Where are you keeping it?"

"It's not her fault that you trusted a stranger," Maya said, taking slow steps toward Blake. "One of your other runners must have taken it. So back off." My sister, standing up against a drug dealer with a gun. To protect me.

"Look clearly at what your sister is doing," Blake said to Maya. "She's giving you up. That's why the police are out front, *sweetheart*."

Keith had slowly crept his way to Blake and now put his arm around her. "Honey, if the police aren't coming up anytime soon, let's put the gun away. Okay?"

She paused a moment, then hurled the weapon onto the couch. "Fine."

"The police have more guns than we do, anyway," Keith said, nuzzling her neck.

A glimmer of a smile came over Blake without her ever moving her mouth, like a curtain rustling and cracking moonlight into a room.

"Are you going to freak out if I stand up?" I said.

Maya was already there, helping me onto my feet.

"Now," I said, "you're going to let us go downstairs."

"An excellent idea," Keith said. "We'd be thrilled to let you handle the police on your own."

"Abby," Maya said, "I can't go down there."

"Yes, you can," I said, wrapping my arms around her. "I'm the one who brought the police here, remember? Don't worry, I have a plan."

She stared at me nervously. I saw her resisting giving up control, even though we'd lived our whole lives with her in the backseat. But she'd have to continue to trust me, the way I was starting to trust her. She didn't have any other choice.

36.

Out in the hallway, out of that apartment but still away from the police, her first words to me were: "What's going to happen?"

As if I knew. As if I had any idea.

She was so small at that moment. So tiny. Like she'd never be able to live a day without care. She was begging for my selfless protection. But it wouldn't work.

"Alcaraz talked me through it," I tried to explain. "He's got to take you in and ask you questions. There's the issue of running away from the house that one time — we're both going to be in trouble about that — but if you're totally helpful about everything else, they won't press any evasion charges."

"We could claim we were running away from home, that we had no idea the police were coming. That's not *illegal*, right, to run away from home? If we had no idea we were fleeing arrest, or whatever?"

I nodded. The matter of our fleeing was so inconsequential compared to what was about to happen. "So we get in his car and go down to the station," I said. "And he'll ask you questions."

"Will you be there?"

"I'll ask them to let me in, if you'd like me there."

"Yes. I really would. And Dad?"

"I'm eighteen, so I can serve as your guardian. He doesn't have to be there, if you don't want him to be. You have to tell them very clearly that you don't trust your parents to represent your best interests."

"I don't. I just want you."

I looked down the stairwell, at the flickering bare halogen lights forming a line all the way down to the rusty front door. I had to get this all under way before my resolve broke. "We go out that door, and it's over."

She nodded. Her lips had almost disappeared, they were that gray. She was terrified.

"How high are you?" I asked. I wasn't sure if the police would test her for drugs.

"Not much," she said. "Mostly I'm scared. Will you hold my hand?"

I took it. It was cold, her fingers thinner and smaller than my own.

"First," she said, "I want a jacket. I left my green jacket here the other day. Could you grab it for me? It's on the chair by the couch."

Typical. I entered Keith and Blake's apartment one last time and got her jacket.

We rode to the station in silence. Jamison was in the passenger seat, wearing his blues this time. There weren't any handcuffs involved, but I was well aware of the pair dangling from his waist, of the gun at his hip, of the Plexiglas and metal separating us criminals in the backseat from the officers in front.

Maya never let go of my hand. In fact, by the time we'd pulled into the station and parked she was leaning heavily against me, like Cody does when she's sick. It made my heart quake that Maya had been so reduced, that she was changing into a stronger person in the long term but right now was exhausted and confused and in need of my help.

I pulled her hand up to my lips and kissed it.

She was doomed.

37.

That night. Where were you cut?"

Maya shook her head stubbornly. "I don't know what you're talking about. Honestly, I don't."

"Your blood. We found it on one of the murder weapons, intermingled with Jefferson's. That's impossible unless you'd been cut, as well as him," Jamison said. He slammed the table, which reverberated through the interrogation room.

Maya looked at me. I shrugged back, almost imperceptibly. You'd have to know me as well as my sister did to notice it. I'd only been allowed in the room on the condition that I not communicate with Maya. Which was fine, since I didn't know what to tell her, anyway.

"We'll search you if we need to," Alcaraz chimed in.

"You won't find anything," Maya said. She was starting to get angry. That was good.

"Would you prefer to do this without me here?" I offered to Alcaraz. "I can wait in another room or something." Our parents were right outside. Maya was allowed to have one of them with her, but she chose me instead. She refused to have Dad come in, even though he was a lawyer.

"I'm conducting this," Jamison growled. "And you'll stay seated. You're both suspects in my book."

"Choose your battles, man," Maya said with familiar

acidity. "You're really going to try to bring something against my *sister*?"

I stared back at him, imperturbable. I had to get him to lose control of the interrogation I needed him to make a wrong step.

"You'd do best to cooperate, both of you," Alcaraz said.

"Fire away," I said.

"Are you aware, Maya, of the list of evidence stacked against you?"

"I didn't kill Jefferson, so whatever you have won't hold up in court," she said.

"It's all very conclusive, actually. I can promise you right now that no jury in America would find you innocent."

She didn't budge. We'd watched enough TV to recognize a detective pushing for a confession. Maya was about to say she wouldn't say any more without a lawyer, I knew it. All that was stopping her was the fact that I hadn't suggested it already. She assumed I had some master plan. Which I did, of course. Though it was quite different from what she expected.

"I'm not overstating the case," Jamison said, as though he'd read our minds. "There's no trick to this conversation, no hidden manipulation going on. You'll find out how strong my case is soon enough. Let's begin, shall we? First, Maya: the murder weapon. We found it a short way off from the body. And your blood is on it. "

"That's impossible. You've done DNA testing?" Maya asked.

"Not yet. But it's a fairly uncommon type, B negative. Which is the same as yours. DNA results will come back eventually. We're very confident it will be a match."

"Still, other people could have my blood type. Like my sister."

"I'm A positive, actually," I said. "We tested it in a bio lab once."

Maya glared at me indignantly.

"Second," Jamison continued, "we have your confession that you were there. That you struck him."

"Lightly," Maya said. "I struck him very lightly."

"Third, there's the matter of your tattoo. You have a tattoo on your lower back that you had covered up the very night Jefferson Andrews was killed, no? One that used to be his name? It will be easy for us to make out the old tattoo. UV light does the trick very simply."

"How do you know about that?" Maya whispered, staring into the table. I could watch her mind race — why would Keith or Blake tell the police about the tattoo cover-up? And when?

"This isn't the time for you to ask questions," he said. "Concentrate on answering, please."

"What kind of moron would I have to be," Maya said, "to get his tattoo covered up the same night that you're saying I killed him? That would be so stupid. I'd say that only proves even more that I didn't do it."

"Interesting logic, Miss Goodwin. Getting the tattoo covered up is so incriminating that it becomes proof of your innocence. I'm not sure if the court will accept your reasoning quite as easily."

She was nearly hyperventilating. I watched her shirt flutter, a little triangle of cloth at her collar trembling as if there were a breeze in the room.

"How would my blood get on a stupid bottle?"

"A bottle?" Jamison asked.

I closed my eyes and pressed the heels of my palms against my face.

"Yes," Maya said. "I hit him with an old whiskey bottle that was there."

"Really. What did you do with the bottle?"

"I left it."

"No," Jamison said. "You're lying to me. We didn't find a whiskey bottle anywhere near the crime scene."

"Then maybe she didn't kill him," I said.

"I want my dad in here," Maya whispered.

"What did she say?" Jamison said.

"Nothing, she's fine," I said. "Don't make this any worse," I whispered to Maya. "Just cooperate. Tell the truth. If you only start calling for him now, then you look guilty."

"You have the right to an attorney, I informed you about that before we began our conversation," Jamison said, over-enunciating toward the recorder in the middle of the table. "You've said you don't trust your parents to represent your interests in this matter, and have designated your sister as your adult representative. Your rights in the matter have previously been made clear."

"Tell him the truth, Maya, it's as simple as that," I said.

"I hit him with a *bottle*," Maya said defiantly. "I'm sure of it."

"You were high. Extremely high. So high that you couldn't remember taking Jefferson's car." Maya looked at me sharply. "So I don't think we can trust your memories on this," Jamison continued. "You hit him with a rock. Not a bottle. A rock. Forensics has come back conclusively. You picked it up, bludgeoned him with it, then threw it away. You probably meant to throw it in the water, but you came up short. We found it right by the edge, in a recent search. And it didn't have just his blood on it. It had yours as well."

Maya chewed her lip for a few moments, working through the rapidly changing situation. I wondered how long it would take for her to put everything together, if it would happen during this interrogation or later.

Jamison continued, "There's more evidence, of course."

"Go on," I said. "Let him go on, Maya." She stared at me crazily.

"There's the matter of the security camera. We have footage from the gas station across from the high school of you vacuuming Jefferson Andrews's car early in the morning after he died. What were you trying to clean out?"

Maya stared back at him. She truly had no idea what he was talking about.

I stared at the doorknob that I'd have to turn to flee the examination room, silver except where the friction of hands had revealed a ring of copper color.

Alcaraz sighed. "Are you really going to pretend you don't know what we're talking about?"

"I'm not pretending," Maya said desperately, swatting at her hair. She was still high, I realized. I wondered if the detectives had noticed yet. "Oh god, oh god. Abby, tell him I don't know what he's talking about."

"None of this makes any sense," I said stiffly.

"Do you want some water?" Jamison asked, pouring a plastic cup of water from a jug at the center of the table and pushing it toward Maya.

"He's making this up, isn't he?" Maya said. "Show us this video you claim to have."

Jamison looked meaningfully at me. "I don't need to show you."

Maya swatted at her hair again and peered at me from under the tangled mass. "What is he *talking about*?" she asked.

"I'm sorry," I said.

"What are you sorry about?"

Jamison sighed and looked at me apologetically. "Abby turned in the security footage to us, Maya. She can tell you what it shows," Jamison said.

"And how did you get it?" she asked me, blinking in incomprehension. Her expression had turned into something awful, a black shroud.

"Don't worry about it," I said.

"How can you tell me not to worry about it?" Maya asked. "What could there possibly be not to worry about?" Her words didn't make sense and made perfect sense at the same time. My heart was making shivery motions in my chest, pumping cold to my limbs. "I didn't do it," Maya said emphatically to Jamison.

A pitiful silence filled the room.

"Then who did?" he said.

Maya stared at the wood grain of the table and then, slowly, raised her eyes to look at me.

For a glittering moment, our gazes locked. She was utterly helpless. Then I spoke. "Show him the key," I said.

"What key?"

"You know exactly what key I mean."

"I really don't. Abby, what's going on?"

"The key in your jacket pocket."

Stunned, she reached into the pockets of her jacket and started when her fingers contacted something. She started trembling and shaking her head. Slowly, she pulled out her hand.

A key.

Jefferson's car key.

38.

My memory of the rest of that brief purgatory in the police station is vague. Maya convulsed once, stopped being able to speak, stared deeply into her knuckles, and then broke into keening sobs. That brought my parents busting in. They saw my distress, Jamison's satisfaction, Maya's tears, and made all the necessary connections. That Maya was screaming out that I'd betrayed her only made her seem more desperate and unhinged, painted her more fully as someone mad enough to have killed Jefferson.

When Jamison brought out the handcuffs and slid them over Maya's wrists, Dad lost it, became a red teary beast raging through the police station.

Mom and I turned to vapor and floated to a quiet place in the front hall. Maya was gone and Dad had ceased to be a human. We held each other and cradled the heavy emptiness between us.

The ride back home: Imagine the most awkward family moment you can, then take the awkward and replace it with something equally uncomfortable but blacker. A big gaping hole of a feeling. Thoughts racing and going nowhere. Maya was in custody, and there was only one way things would go from here. Our parents would have to finally put to rest any of their doubts that Maya really was Jefferson's killer. I wasn't looking forward to that conversation. It wouldn't happen for some time, I knew. My house would be queasily quiet for days.

Once they got inside, Mom and Dad huddled around the phone, setting up the legal war plan. I glided up to my room. They wouldn't be bothering me for a while. For a blissful and painful stretch of time, I'd have nothing to do but disappear.

I slid into my bed, pulled a protesting Cody under the sheets beside me, tucked the comforter around my head like a mummy, and slipped into the fullest sleep I'd had in ages.

TUESDAY, JUNE 4

39.

Brian and I wound up assigned to the same therapist. Guess there's only one shrink nearby equipped to deal with teenagers who are going through stuff on our scale. I told my mom and dad that I definitely didn't need anyone that hard-core, that I had looked her up online and was positive I didn't have post-traumatic stress disorder and that the last thing I wanted to do was jabber about my sister to a woman who would frown in concern and take notes in her notepad about how brave I was. But my parents knew the distance that had sprung up in me, that I wasn't talking to them or spending time with any of my friends.

Cheyenne and I had started treating each other like strangers. She'd tried to get me to open up at first, but I couldn't. And when I glazed over while she was telling me about her mom's clinginess at the thought of her going away to college, Cheyenne stopped speaking to me all over again. The rest of the kids at school weren't much better — Rose tried to smear me with what Maya had done. It didn't stick, because I didn't care. But I guess it looked like everything was taking a toll on me, and my parents made their diagnosis. So I spent two hours every Tuesday and Thursday on I-75, the forty-five minutes of therapy in between spent with a trauma specialist, reciting a story I now know by heart.

There was a big silk ficus in the doctor's waiting room, and it draped over one of the seats, practically hiding it away. People sat in that chair only if the rest of the waiting room was full, but Brian always gravitated to it. Since his appointment was after mine, I'd gotten used to opening the door after I finished and seeing him hidden behind the plant, eating candy from the freebie tray, deep in a paperback about hot women in chain-mail bikinis. The first few times we avoided each other so intently that it looked like we'd had some breakup in our past. The receptionist raised her eyebrow at us.

One time, though, Brian didn't have his book with him. He very consciously met my eyes when I came out. I said hey, and so did he. I kept walking toward the door.

"I don't have an appointment today," he said.

"Why are you here, then?" I asked, reluctantly stopping.

"Let's get a smoothie next door. I've been meaning to try that place."

We sat at a rusty wire table at the edge of the parking lot, him armed with Chocolate Banana, me with Mango Madness. I could barely taste my smoothie; he'd driven here just to see me, and it had my mind racing.

"What's the word from Maya?" he asked.

"Maya doesn't talk to me," I said. "You probably heard they set bail way high because of the whole flight-risk thing, so she's not home. I'm almost glad the trial's in a few weeks. We'll get everything settled and stuff."

"Does she get to visit with anyone? Like, have one of those phone conversations across a plastic wall?"

"Yeah. But I let my parents take care of that. I don't know if I'm up for it. She's still so angry at me for turning her in. Like I had a choice."

He paused. His features twisted; I could see him debating whether to ask me something. Maybe he was going to protest that I *did* have a choice.

He finally spoke. "Are you sure she did it?" he asked.

The parking lot was full of cars, but there weren't any people around. We had that pure privacy you only get in public places.

"How can anyone be sure about anything?" I replied carefully. For all I knew, this whole conversation might be repeated to Brian's parents and their lawyers.

"I know you gave them my drawings. Or told my mom where they were. I was mad at you. But I don't think I am anymore. I mean, I get that you were trying to protect Maya. Sometimes I wish I'd been able to protect Jefferson. And a lot of the time I feel guilty that I never would've tried."

"It's not your fault," I said.

"I know. But still, with the trial and everything else, and the way everyone is making it like Jefferson was this big hero — maybe he was, and I couldn't see it. I wish I'd loved him more. Like you love Maya. You did so much for her."

"You don't understand," I said. "Sure, there are times when I love Maya. But there are a lot of times when I hate her, too. And that's okay."

"Thank you," Brian whispered. "That kind of thing might seem obvious to you, but it helps to hear it."

I could tell he felt better. But I couldn't feel anything at all.

In another life, if I were someone completely different, I would have been able to console him more. There might have been a future involved. Not romantic — just *connected*. But that was the thing about our connection. All we'd ever have was the past.

MONDAY, JUNE 24

40.

Maya was in court quickly; the presumed killer of the town's high school star was guaranteed to get a speedy trial. There was really no question of how it was all going to end. There was simply too much evidence stacked against her — the blood, the fact that she'd confessed to being there and striking him, her prior record of petty offenses, that footage of her cleaning out Jefferson's car, her having his car key.

I was called as a witness to corroborate the prosecution's claim that I had informed Maya that Jefferson was meeting up with a girl, and to explain how the video had come to be in my possession. Any accusations of betrayal by Maya — and there had been none recently — had long been dismissed as mad ravings.

"Who was the girl Jefferson was planning to meet up with?" the prosecutor, a middle-aged woman in a rumpled gray suit, asked.

"I don't know. I heard he was going to meet up with someone named Caitlin. Overheard him talking to some buddies. You know." Since it was already an acknowledged fact that Maya had been at the Bend the night Jefferson died, the prosecutor didn't have much more to ask me, and I was able to leave.

I managed not to meet Maya's eyes during my testimony — I was only aware of the fringe of her dyed hair and the edge of the defense table — but as I left the courtroom, I couldn't help but glance at her. She didn't seem haggard or abused; she was being held at a relatively cushy youth ranch nearby. But the expression I saw on her face as I passed through the courtroom will always stay with me. I could have dealt with anger or immense sadness (I deserved the anger, I understood the sadness); I anticipated she might leap to her feet and shout out a desperate accusation (which would only add to the court's impression of her as a crazy loon . . . and maybe lessen her sentence, I'd hoped), but instead, she had this serene expression on. It wasn't like she was pretending not to know me, but rather that she understood me so deeply that she needed to express nothing to me; that she understood that my existence was worth more than hers; that of our two lives, hers was the one that should rightfully be lost, even if unfairly.

I left the courthouse and sat in the sun on the outside steps and stared at the ants swarming the gaps between the stones and thought of her, my sister. Her lost opportunities — the smaller ones she'd missed all her life, by shrugging off schoolwork or connections with family, and the colossal one she'd inevitably lose when the jury returned its verdict: the opportunity to be free at all.

SATURDAY, DECEMBER 21

41.

Maya was sentenced to fifteen years. The fact that she was a young girl who'd been stoned out of her mind prevented the jury from giving her a harsher sentence. She'd be up for review before eight years were over. But still, she was going to be spending a lot of time behind bars.

The last month of summer before I went up to Vanderbilt was the equivalent of a waiting room, endured and then forgotten. Maya asked to see me, but I refused. Mom begged me to visit her, but Dad defended my decision — I think he saw how closely I'd been involved in everything, and that it was better for my mental health that I got some distance, even if from my own sister. He was the one to drive me up to college; Mom still wasn't leaving the house. We had some really great talks on the way; he opened up about how long he'd felt he'd been letting Maya down, how he was arranging for her to take coursework while she was in prison, that he was doing everything he could to have a stable life set up for her once she was eventually released. That was his way of dealing with his guilt.

As for me, I initially decided that I couldn't face seeing Maya behind bars. But she kept on asking for me, until Dad called and soberly said that he didn't think Mom would be able to move on until I finally agreed to see my sister. I was approaching my first set of finals and could have pled organic chemistry homework, but I hated to think of my mom so sad. A reunion with Maya was inevitable, so I agreed to go.

"Your sister needs you," my mother kept saying. And I couldn't find a way to say, *I'm the last thing she needs.*

I'd already planned to drive down from Tennessee for winter break, and I changed my plan so I'd go straight to the juvenile prison. I couldn't risk going home first, sitting with my parents and letting myself come up with excuses not to see her. So I drove fifteen hours straight, wired on caffeine and candy, and pulled into the prison parking lot at dawn.

As planned, Cheyenne was waiting for me. She was home on break from Miami, and a few weeks earlier we'd started e-mailing again. I wrote her that I was finally going to face my sister, and she immediately said she'd come support me. She switched from a stranger back to a best friend, just like that, the moment I really needed her. Even after six months of silence, she'd gone back to being the person I could most be myself with. Seeing her waiting for me in the parking lot was therapy in a way my therapist had never been.

She was dressed in usual Cheyenne style, pilly peacoat over a patterned shirt. It was so reassuring that she was still *her.* Full minutes went by before we stopped hugging each other. I hadn't made any real friends at Vanderbilt, not yet. I couldn't bring myself to go out. So it was such a relief to be with someone who knew and loved me.

We'd agreed that she'd wait for me outside, and then drive us to lunch as soon as I came out, picking my car back up afterward. I couldn't start asking about her life and delay seeing Maya, so I stepped away as soon as our hug ended.

She stopped me, though, and pulled something out of her car. Coffee and donuts.

I thanked her and went inside, where I gave my name and ID and passed through prison security. I was led down a hallway with a red line painted down the center to separate visitors from criminals. A guard ushered me through a door and into a room very similar to the Xavier High cafeteria, all cinder block and shiny paint. Maya was there waiting for me. She was still drawn out and wiry, but six months without drugs gave her a newly robust color. She had health and hardship written all over her. We were sitting at a folding table covered in imitation wood. Add a box of milk and orange pizza, and it could have been like the first day at a new school. But the guard ten feet away killed the illusion that life was anything near normal.

"Hi," I said, plopping the donuts on the table.

She replied without hesitation: "Hi, *Caitlin*."

The world stopped for a moment. I'd almost sat down but now I froze, hanging ridiculously in the space over the chair. My heart dropped: Maybe she really thought that was my name. Maybe she was now fully and completely insane. I caught a glimpse of my reflection in the window: hysterical, weary.

"What did you call me?" I asked.

"Never mind. Have a seat."

I could think of no option but to obey her. "You look good," I said, fiddling with the coffee cup.

She ignored the compliment. "One thing you get tons of here," she said, "is time to think. To put things together."

"Do you even want me to be here? Because you haven't even asked me how I'm doing, and I have no idea what you're talking about."

"I don't care whether you admit it. The fact that you've spent so long avoiding me makes me think you'll never face the truth. But I'm going to tell you what I now know is true, beyond any doubt."

My hands were clenched together, slick and cold. "Maya, I don't think —"

"You fell for Jefferson the moment he entered our house, didn't you?"

I almost answered her question — for a split second I thought it would have felt good to spill the truth. But cool reason took over and I stayed silent and sat with my shock.

No. I fell for him long before he ever entered our house. Whenever he was consciously flirting, he got this curve to one side of his mouth, like someone posing a riddle. Nothing about him wasn't essential: Everything was messy, but nothing was out of place.

"Are you going to say anything?" Maya pressed. "Because I'm positive that you were sleeping with him."

No, Maya. It was way more than that. You have no idea.

"Maya," I said. "Think how crazy that sounds."

Why had I figured I'd be any different, that he'd immortalize the flash of connection we had? I was just another one of his girls. Somewhere, I'd always suspected it.

"Abby," Maya said quietly, "I'm in jail. Nothing's going to change that. It's not like anything you say will let me walk free. So at least give me the benefit of a little honesty."

"I haven't lied to you," I said.

When I was with him, it was like some intense woman inside me burst out of a paper shell. Jefferson had coaxed it out, with that mouth of his. Those fingers. When we were together, I'd been consumed with thoughts that I'd betrayed you. How ironic, when eventually I'd betray you far worse.

"I found a picture of you. With him. I jacked it from Jefferson's stuff once. Do you remember the moment? You were on Jefferson's bed. You'd been crying."

I remembered that moment well, though I'd had no idea that I was being photographed. He'd told me he wouldn't sleep with me anymore, that I had gotten too serious and he'd only been into us when it was all more carefree. I'd promised him I didn't expect anything from him, that I could be casual and fun again. But I'd been bawling. In the end I buried my head away. I'd thought he'd been sitting there dejected, but he'd been taking pictures. He had a grin on his face: Mission accomplished. Another girl used and then booted. More proof of his power. I'd finally looked up to see Jefferson shirtless and staring into the mirror, feeling his six-pack and taking more pictures. In another few minutes, I'd be out of there and on the other side of town, shrieking and sobbing in my bedroom so hard that my parents would hear and come knocking. No one had ever rejected me like that. Or rejected me at all, really.

"If you'd had anything like that," I said, "you would have brought it to the police. You're flat-out lying. I didn't come here for this."

"Did you happen to notice that I was basically homeless? It was a little hard to keep track of my belongings," Maya said bitterly. Then the sarcasm dropped and a note of sadness entered her voice. "I lost it. And in a way, that wasn't you in the picture. It was Caitlin. That's the name you told Jefferson to call you, so if you came up on his phone, I wouldn't know it was my own sister."

When he cast me out of his bedroom that last time, left me dirty and alone, I needed him to pay. He'd gone straight back to you. To hurt me, or for more obscure reasons. Either way, I wanted him to suffer. I also hoped to save you from him. So I used the last card I had, that final meeting I'd gotten Jefferson to agree to, and told you about it. I had you show up instead of me. I supplied the name Caitlin so he'd know, as soon as you said it, who'd sent you to him. I'd take his toy away before he was finished with it, and save you from heartbreak at the same time. And I'd watch from the trees. If it didn't all go the way I wanted it to go, I'd step in and confront him myself.

But you were wrong about one thing: I hadn't been the one originally to come up with the name. It had been Jefferson. Does it matter, though? We'd both betrayed you.

"I can see you know what I'm saying. It's all over your face. Listen, Abby, I get why you killed him," Maya said.

"Believe me, I get it. But why you had to frame me, I haven't figured out. Maybe you've held a grudge against me for years, for putting you and Mom and Dad through so much crap. Can't say I'd blame you for that. I sort of deserve what's happened to me. But I also deserve to know the truth about it, don't you think?"

She was remorseful more than angry. I hadn't anticipated that, and it caught me off guard. I took a few moments before responding. "Maya," I said evenly, "I don't think I deserve to have wild accusations thrown at me. Would you give this up so we can catch up?"

"Catch up?! Are you serious? You watched me, didn't you?" she said, stabbing the tabletop with a finger. "You saw me confront him. You saw me hit him. He *wanted* me to. He was enjoying it. I bet you saw that, too. I cut him bad with that bottle when it slipped from my fingers. So I flipped and ran away. And that's when you appeared."

"Is that so?"

You're exactly right.

"And then he saw you and attacked you. You defended yourself."

Jefferson. He was still kneeling there, bright in the headlights of his car, holding his face. The things he was saying about you: You were the biggest whore of all time, you would pay, he'd get you and your slutty friends one by one and take all of you down.

Because I'd once loved him, I hated him. So much. I hated how he was a user, how other people adored him for it. How he abused everyone and seized on any insecurities. And there he was,

293

vulnerable in front of me. With no idea I was there. It dawned on me: No one in the world had any idea I was there.

Until I saw you hit him, I hadn't ever considered it was possible to wound Jefferson, that he was mortal. But the sight of his blood pushed me to new places. I could hurt him so much worse than I'd ever imagined. There was a rock under my feet. I pulled it up from the muck and hurled it.

It was sharp and heavy and filthy, and I hit the part of his skull where you had already parted the flesh, took that seam and ripped it open. There must be some huge blood vessel that runs over your temple; it erupted all over. I remember big globs of blood spraying in the headlights. He was blinded by his own blood, staggered backward. I picked the rock back up and hit him again. And again. It was slick and kept falling from my fingers, but I'd find it and come after him again. He was screaming, thrashing around. I hit him one last time, and he lost his balance and fell back through the trees. I heard branches breaking, farther and farther away, until his fall stopped with a splash.

I stood there in the clearing for a while, heaving and retching as I slowly came back to my senses. I couldn't hear anything from below but an awful stillness.

"It *was* self-defense, right?" Maya asked.

I couldn't bring myself to go confirm there really was a dead body down there; I hoped I'd find the strength come morning. But I knew how hard I'd hit him. I knew the sounds his skull made as it split.

Maya stared at me incredulously. "Would you at least react? I'm getting nothing from you."

I thought back to that AP psych class, when Mr. Wachsberger had described sociopaths as charismatic people with powerful reasoning and no emotional compass. I'd stared at Jefferson, waiting for him to flinch.

He wasn't the one who ought to have flinched.

Maybe I am a sociopath. My life has been a series of options weighed and selected, with consequences leading to more sets of options. Anyone hearing what happened wouldn't know it, but so often my emotions simply don't match the events.

"As soon as you stop being crazy," I said coolly, "I'll start reacting."

"That was you in the car," she said.

"What are you getting at?"

"Where were you that night, then?"

"At home. In bed."

First thing I did was turn off the engine and headlights. Worst possibility was that someone would chance upon me before I'd figured out what I was going to do, and his running car was like a lighthouse beacon. I wiped off the rock I'd killed him with and wrapped it in stray newspaper and placed it in the backseat. I shut myself in his car and locked the doors. It smelled like his detergent and his sweat. I remembered the same smell from wrestling with him after we had sex one time, the smell of it especially strong on the corded muscles at the base of his neck.

What to do? I could call 911 right away, report the accident so someone would come help him, in case he was alive. But I'd attacked him, and calling 911 would mean turning myself in. If I didn't call, his absence would be noticed within a day. The Andrewses would start a search. They'd track down Maya. Then they'd track me down. Or would they? No one knew about my obsession with Jefferson — I was too embarrassed that I'd fallen for someone so cruel to let any of my friends know.

"When did you make the plan to frame me?" Maya said.

I stared back at her.

I wish I'd known the full extent of Brian's weirdness back then — I might have made him my target from the start. This all would have ended so differently. But the only person I could think of pinning everything on was you.

Part of me even thought you deserved it.

"Look," Maya said. "I get it. I'd basically checked out from our family. We both knew there was no way I was going to be getting a diploma anytime soon. If fate had gone another direction, it could have been me who killed him. And if one of us was going to lose her future, why not have it be the one who barely had a future to start with?"

She was trying to console me — but only to spur me to confess. "Maya," I said. "I don't know what to tell you. You're the most important person in my life. But at the same time, it's not like what you're saying is true. I've spent huge chunks of my life worrying about you. I . . . I don't know what I'm trying to say."

"You loved me and wanted to be rid of me at the same time."

Yes. Of course. No one ever accused you of stupidity, Maya.

It was inevitable that our family would lose you, anyway, so why not nudge you to run away? If you suddenly went missing, you'd automatically become the main suspect. You'd hit him — and hard enough that you'd have to doubt your role in his death. You were totally high, anyway. If you disappeared, I'd be safe. We'd both be safe.

"If it wasn't self defense, then maybe you'd had it planned for days. That you'd kill him — or maybe you had someone else kill him, like Cheyenne, I don't know — and then you'd get me to run away."

I hadn't planned it for days. I hadn't planned it at all. But once it all started, there were two crucial steps: first, to implicate you. And second, yes, to get you to run away.

The implicating . . . you'd lost your sweatshirt during the fight with Jefferson. It wasn't much, but it was a start. I felt around until I found it, threw it in the backseat. I also kept the bottle you'd struck Jefferson with, careful to handle it only with the sweatshirt sleeve. Rock, bottle, sweatshirt. I started up the car and headed out.

I'd figured you'd call a friend to pick you up; I didn't know yet that you'd lost your phone.

Maya went on. "All that mattered to you was that I wouldn't turn to Mom and Dad for help. I'd have to depend on you."

I stopped home, making sure I parked down the block so I wouldn't wake our parents, and took a long shower. I hid the whiskey bottle and rock in the cluttered garage so that I'd have Jefferson's blood sample to plant once I'd figured out how I wanted to do it.

"Ernie and the police were wrong about who they thought they saw in the footage at the gas station. That whole video thing was some random girl in a car that looked like Jefferson's. That was all pure luck for you."

Oh, Maya. I put your sweatshirt on and drove to Ernie's gas station. I faced away from the cameras. I pretended to vacuum. Everyone always said we had the same body type. If I'd ever been a real suspect, the police might have realized that it could have been me dressed up as you. But at that point, you were the only one on their radar.

I drove the car downtown and left it in one of the areas where I knew you loved to hang out. Near Medusa's Den, where all the downtown street kids killed time. I got a cab home. I hid the key to Jefferson's car — I figured it would come in handy one day.

I couldn't personally come forward with any of the evidence against you, of course, without looking suspicious myself. So I had to let it be discovered in the course of other people's lives. Let the police come to Ernie, or wait for him to look over his security footage himself. Let Jefferson's car turn up a few days into the investigation, with your sweatshirt in the back — the same one from the footage.

Up until then, I'd been treating Maya's accusations as unworthy of any consideration. But I had to know: "Do you have any evidence for any of this?"

Her eyes narrowed. "We'll get to that."

I didn't sleep that night. How could I? By morning it was destroying me, the fact that I'd never seen Jefferson's dead body. What if he'd survived, if I was risking your freedom for nothing? I had to know. So I went for a run. I went to the place I most dreaded and was most drawn to.

I found the body. I confirmed to myself that he was dead. Seeing his corpse was horrific. Having been the one to kill him didn't lessen the shock.

Your cell phone was a wild card. I didn't know you'd lost it that night. I guess I could have left it there for the police to find. But since the phone was missing, I had no way to contact you. I needed your friends' numbers.

"I never set out trying to get you jailed. So drop it," I said.

And it's true. I wanted you to be long gone by the time the police put the case together. You'd be nailed, sure, but hidden away and untraceable. To get everything started, though, I'd have to locate you and convince you to run. So I started calling your friends.

"Once you managed to track me down," Maya said, "you realized I wasn't sure about how badly I'd hurt Jefferson. You tried to make me believe that I might have done it. You'd always been my responsible older sister, so I was totally open to your suggestions. You played me so easily."

"That's too much. Really."

The fact that you'd had your Jefferson tattoo covered up before going to meet with him was a revelation, too. But it was a very welcome one — once that fact came out, it would only make the case against you stronger. I nabbed the bloody bandage Cody found in the trash. Having a blood sample for you would prove useful later. I'd considered keeping your cell phone, too, but realized giving it to you would prove my loyalty even as it allowed me to keep closer tabs on you.

I hadn't predicted you'd want to stay with Veronica, but that suited me fine. Veronica wouldn't be stupid enough to let you remain there, but would move you to some other isolated location. And she was a distant enough relation to our own family that I didn't have to worry about the police knocking on her door before we'd figured out where to hide you permanently.

At that point, it was a matter of getting anyone but me (thank you, Cheyenne) to place the tip to the police, and let the ball start its inevitable roll toward you.

As if hearing my thoughts, Maya said, "Our parents, Cheyenne, and Veronica — it didn't take much to keep them all pointed in my direction, did it?"

"If you're not going to give this up and start talking to me as you should to a sister who's been looking out for you all year, I'm leaving."

She looked up at me slyly, like this was the latest in a series of entirely predictable reactions. "Don't you want to know what else I've pieced together?"

"You're ridiculous," I said.

"You won't guess who's been to see me recently," Maya said. "Brian."

I never would have predicted Brian would enter the story. But after I discovered him skipping school that day, I soon realized what a perfect suspect he would make. More likely than you, even. Those creepy weapons, that cold-hearted attitude to his own brother, expressed so publicly at the assembly. And if the police turned toward him, I wouldn't have to live with the guilt of having framed you.

"Who cares that Brian's been to see you?" I said. "People are even less inclined to believe him than they are you."

"I care about Brian," Maya said. "And he actually believes that you care about him, too."

I'd worked on Brian. But in the meantime, it was in my best interest to keep you a crazy runaway in everyone's eyes. Because then you were dependent on me. The more control I had over you, and the lower everyone's opinion of your mental state, the more chance I had of stopping you from coming back and getting yourself captured.

While I was tracking down your location, I discovered the message from Blake, trying to get you to come meet her. Blake, of course, was trying to get her drug money back. Keith hadn't told her about Jefferson's death, I guess because he knew she would go as ballistic as she eventually did. That you'd been running money for them came as a shock — your life was more complicated than I'd thought, and from then on, it would take all my concentration to keep the variables in order.

By then, my friendship with Brian was in full swing. That laptop picture of Jefferson and you together — I showed it to Brian and then wrecked the laptop, because I knew there had to be other evidence on that computer that could incriminate me. Let Brian's suspicions aid the case against you, and let the destruction of Jefferson's laptop prevent the police from linking him to me.

The first interrogation with Alcaraz and Jamison, I sent our parents away so I could talk more freely, fudge whatever minor truths I needed to in order to better position you. I also wanted to steer the police into making me their main communication link to you, instead of my parents — that way, I could control the information you received as conditions changed. I knew Mom and Dad wouldn't approve of my taking on that kind of responsibility — good thing I'd kept them from being there to hear about the offer.

As for our parents, I had to keep them thinking of you as guilty. If they started to suspect you were actually innocent, they'd stop at nothing to free you. But I could also rely on their sense of justice. If their daughter really had killed someone, they'd do their best for you, but they'd also be sure you went to trial.

"You're not looking into my eyes," Maya said. "I'm going through hell facing you with all this, and you won't even look me in the eyes."

Oh, poor Maya.

But yes, poor Maya. I felt a sudden surge of sympathy and looked at her. "If it's so hellish, why don't you stop putting us both through this?"

"I hid those drugs so good. You moved them so Dad would find them easily. At least admit that much."

"Do you honestly think, in the middle of a murder investigation, that I would go around handling your drugs?"

I'd been loud, and the word *drugs* rang out in the hall. The guard glanced over. Maya made a motion for me to keep my voice down.

You're right, Maya. I could have gotten rid of your drugs for you, but instead I moved them under the bed, where our father would be more likely to find them. It was another nail in the coffin.

"You waited until you had the trap set perfectly, and then you suggested I come back. And I believed you. You must think I'm such a fool, don't you?"

"You offered to come back, remember?"

It wasn't a trap. For the longest time, I wanted you never to return, to keep you far away so we both could be safe. But at the same time that I was getting to know Brian better, you started hinting that you wanted to come back. I couldn't talk you out of it. All I had were those sporadic online conversations, and you kept cutting them short. I realized I'd have to start burning the candle at both ends, implicate you and Brian simultaneously. If you stayed away, I could keep you as the prime suspect. If you really came back, though, I'd have to throw all my weight into directing the investigation toward Brian. If worse came to worst, I'd have two suspects the police would turn to long before thinking of me. It only made my position safer, even as it made my maneuvering that much more complicated.

"How you got your hands on Brian's pictures, I have no idea."

I sneaked in his room to get my bracelet back from Jefferson's box of treasures, so no one would link me to him. That's when I found the drawings. For Mrs. Andrews to suspect her own son was an ideal turn of events.

Of course, I had my compunctions. If my plan succeeded, Brian would wrongfully go to prison. So I hesitated. But telling Mom about the pictures was so simple, so natural. I couldn't resist. And then Brian was suddenly suspect number one. And I thought you were safe again.

With Brian the police's main target, I could bring you back. As long as you returned quietly and didn't let too many people know too soon, it would be safe.

My position wasn't as safe as I'd thought it was, though. Brian leveled those "ridiculous" accusations in the park, claiming I could have been the killer. Veronica brought up that story about the toucan, that I sometimes did the immoral thing in the name of good. I started getting nervous. The edges of the tale I was weaving had begun to unravel.

But then things started to look up. Veronica admitted that she really believed you did it. And Ernie contacted me about the video.

I'd imagined he'd send the recording to the police, or that they would have asked him for it during their investigation. That would have been fine. But Ernie called me. When he offered to destroy the recording, I smooth-talked him into giving it to me. Right then, Brian was still the main suspect, so I didn't plan on doing anything with the recording, but I knew it'd be essential to have that evidence at my disposal. So I got it from Ernie, to send to the police once it was necessary. Which I eventually did, of course.

"Abby!" Maya said. "Admit it: You had a trap set for me when you talked me into returning."

"It's like I explained at the trial. I brought you home because I thought you were innocent."

Which is true — I knew you were innocent. But once you were back, Dad, realizing that having you home without telling the police would only make the situation worse, called in Alcaraz.

They interrogated us, and then I realized it — it would always be dangerous to have you around; you were inevitably going to remain a suspect . . . and I had the perfect opportunity to get you back on the run. That night, when I got up, I came back and told you Dad was outside waiting for the police to come arrest you. But he hadn't betrayed you — after the day's drama, he simply couldn't sleep and was pacing the house. He wasn't out front at all. I woke you up and we fled. I made sure we were noisy enough that Dad found us. Seeing him staggering toward us only confirmed your fear. We ran away, along the creek.

Keith and Blake's was as safe a sanctuary as I could imagine. It was their whole aim in life, after all, to stay under the police's radar.

But then it took a turn for the worse. Alcaraz was onto me. That meeting I had with him at Veronica's was horrifying. That Cheyenne had turned me in. That the police knew I had hidden you away with our stepgrandmother. That they were onto something fishy in every single thing I'd been involved in.

I panicked. The protectiveness I'd started feeling toward you vanished. After I left Veronica's and before I went back to find you, I picked up the rock from its hiding place. The blood from your tattoo bandage was hardened and black, but by mixing it with water, I was able to smear some of it on. I brought it to Alcaraz, saying I'd found it in your bedroom and had been too intent on protecting you to turn it in earlier. I could have used the bottle, but Brian had already let slip that the police thought Jefferson's fatal wounds had come from a rock. I said I was willing to face the consequences, but Alcaraz said having the murder weapon was the most *important thing and he'd overlook my having withheld evidence. That was when I told him about your tattoo cover-up, too. Through it all, he never suspected I could have been the one to kill Jefferson.*

Alcaraz and I arranged that I would go get you so I could turn you in to the police. But you and I got wrapped up in Blake and Keith's drama, of course. Blake started throwing out those wild accusations. But what she was trying to accomplish was too little, and too late.

I had you in my grasp. And I turned you in.

You thought I was leading you to safety. But I'd planted Jefferson's car key in your jacket. I'd had it since the night I killed him and was waiting for the right opportunity to use it. Even though you were wary, you had faith in me to the end. Trusting me was your fatal mistake, and you committed it over and over.

It was cold in the visiting chamber, and I saw Maya shiver in her baggy orange sweatshirt. "Will they let me go get you something warm to wear from my car?" I asked.

Maya shook her head. She'd stopped accusing me and was only staring at me grimly. She was gone, and it was so much worse than when she'd been fighting with me.

"What was that thing you were going to tell me, what you thought you had on me?" I asked.

She shook her head savagely. If she'd had any tears left in her, I might have seen some. "This is not how I imagined this going," she finally said quietly. "You're not going to offer me anything, are you?"

"Are you done?" I asked, keeping my voice level even though my heart was quaking. "Mom and Dad are expecting me."

"You made your choice," Maya said. "I don't totally blame you." She gave me a defiant look, like she'd taken some unknown high ground, that in some obscure way I was the one who'd been defeated.

No, Maya. You're the one in prison.

I stood up, and the guard started walking over to bring her back to her cell. I couldn't resist one last try: "You're not going to tell me what that thing is you think you have on me?"

She didn't look resigned or angry. Instead she flashed me — shockingly, impossibly, mind-flutteringly — a smile. It was the same unknowable expression she had given me back when we were kids fighting in the backseat of the car: *I have something on you. I am larger. I reach further.*

"Nothing," she said. "You left me nothing." The smile never left her face as she was escorted away. It was almost as though she was impressed that I'd finally met her level. She was . . . proud.

I passed through the hallways and gates and left the prison. Cheyenne was waiting for me outside, and gave me a long hug. Some thaw happened during that hug. I thought I'd be able to remain in control forever, but suddenly I was sobbing. It was like how, in the food court so long ago, I thought I wouldn't tell Cheyenne about Jefferson's death, and then I couldn't stop myself.

People talk about how guilt works slowly but will eventually destroy you, how a killer will turn himself in years after the crime or will be found hanging from a rafter, a note around his neck describing long-forgotten events from a previous decade. We read that Poe story in class, about the telltale heart beating its accusations against the floorboards. I don't feel any of that. But don't get me wrong. I feel something just as intense, just as heart-filling. I want to be known, and I'm sure I never will be. Nobody knows what I've done.

"Cheyenne," I said.

"Shh."

I pulled back and looked her in the eyes. "No, Cheyenne, I need to tell you something."

"No," she said somberly, "you don't need to tell me anything."

"It's about Maya. Something I did, that I have to admit to someone. Something huge."

Cheyenne unlocked the car door. "You don't have to admit it. Because I already know what you're going to say."

She disappeared into the car. I stood there a moment, stunned, and then got in beside her.

She started the car and we were soon on the interstate heading south, to home and holidays and security. Cheyenne spoke. "I've had a lot of time to think about what you did. You're still the most important person in the world to me. You've done the cruelest thing anyone could ever imagine, and yet I somehow understand it. But you don't get to vent. You have to sit with it. I'll be here for everything else you need in life, but not that."

My tears vanished. Cheyenne and I drove in silence. She'd figured it all out — but we would never talk about it. That was the cost: I would never be able to live a transparent life. I would never be known.

"This is the real reason you stopped being friends with me for a while, isn't it?" I asked.

Cheyenne didn't answer, just concentrated on the road.

"How did you figure it out?"

"I know you," she said simply.

She and I might have been best friends, but it was Jefferson who'd had my soul. It was Jefferson who had made me forget to speak and to breathe, Jefferson I'd wait three hours in the rain to glimpse. Jefferson who, in the end, had been profounder and more interesting than me and had dumped me for profounder and more interesting girls. Jefferson who, I now realized, I'd become worthy of through the very act of killing him. By framing my sister, becoming someone filthy and exciting and superhuman, I'd become the one girl who might have held his interest.

But he was dead.

I couldn't move. I couldn't look at Cheyenne. I couldn't speak.

And so it was she who spoke to me. "No one will believe Maya. And I won't tell anyone."

She squeezed my arm, and then returned her hand to the wheel.

She couldn't face all of me. She couldn't take on my dark side, like Jefferson had done . . . and lost.

But she knew what I had done. And she was still here with me.

"I could be honest and choose Maya, or I could lie and choose you," she said. "And I choose you."

I stared out at the road.

She chose me.

Acknowledgments

Thanks to all my emailing readers, and to friends and family who read drafts, including Marie Rutkoski, Heather Duffy-Stone, Eric Zahler, and Barbara Schrefer.

As always, thanks to my agent, Richard Pine, and my editor, David Levithan, who yet again showed up at lunch with a great idea for a book.

ELIOT SCHREFER is the author of *The School for Dangerous Girls, Glamorous Disasters,* and *The New Kid.* He lives in New York City and runs quite often, but has yet to discover a body while doing so. He also does not have a sister.

Visit Eliot on the Web at
www.eliotschrefer.com.